When the Dead Weep

Marshall & Blaylock Investigations, Volume 1

JC BLAKE

Published by Redbegga Publishing, 2020.

This is a work of fiction. Similarities to real people, places, or events are entirely coincidental.

WHEN THE DEAD WEEP

First edition. March 31, 2020.

Written by JC BLAKE.

For my family.

PROLOGUE

HMP Portland, Hospital Wing

Psychiatric nurse, Evangeline Maybank, paused at the hospital's secluded entrance, waiting for the barrier to rise, and a shiver ran down her spine that had nothing to do with the chill of the dark November night. From the road, the only indicator of the building's presence was a simple white sign beside the barrier printed with 'HMP Portland'. The vast Victorian edifice of the prison, complete with imposing gothic turrets, was hidden by trees either side of the gravelled drive. "Couldn't get creepier if it tried," Evangeline muttered as she reached the end of the avenue of trees and faced the prison's imposing façade with its wide and gravelled turning circle complete with a redundant water fountain at its centre.

The moon sat as a silver orb behind the turreted, double-storey hospital wing as though pinpointing exactly where she would be incarcerated until the end of her shift. "Bloody nutjob coming here, I am," she grumbled, swinging the car into the staff carpark. "Might as well be locked up with them; I spend more time here than I do at home." At the top of the wide stone steps that led to the prison's main entrance, Evangeline passed beneath the original stone lintel carved with, 'Hospital for the Criminally Insane'.

A pair of kindly blue eyes edged with crow's feet smiled at her as she passed through the entrance doors, and Tony Drinkwater, one of that night's prison officers, stepped out from behind a bank of monitors. "You back again, Eve?" he asked, holding out an oblong tray with one hand whilst adjusting his belt with the other. His belly overhung the tight belt a little less than last week. Too polite to mention Tony's weight loss, she placed her bag in the tray and moved across to the next stage of security. Standing spread-eagled as Henry Babcock ran a security baton over her body, Tony checked the contents of her bag. She had gotten beyond worrying about anything personal the officers may find. After five years of her handbag and body being searched on a daily basis, the security checks had become part of the routine, and she wasn't the type to 'spice it up' like Sally Musgrove. Evangeline had gawped at her night-shift colleague as she had recalled the story of how she had put a certain type of unmentionable adult toy in her bag, 'just to give the officers something to gossip about'.

"No rest for the wicked, Tony" she replied with a tight smile as he handed back her bag. "I need all the overtime I can get."

"Oh? You saving up for something?"

Evangeline's cheeks fizzed with embarrassment, but the lie slipped from her tongue with ease "A holiday in Greece. Colin really wants to go there this year."

"You're too good to that man."

Evangeline gave an exaggerated sigh. "He's worth it." Well, he had been until he'd left her paying the mortgage and the debt racked up in the months before running off with her neighbour. From the list of white goods and furniture bought in Evangeline's name, an entirely new house had been kitted out. The first she had heard about it was when the debt collector's letter arrived threatening to take her to court. There was nothing to be done, no way of proving it wasn't her that had bought it all on credit, and now she was facing financial ruin, about to lose her house, and her reputation, if she didn't keep up the payments negotiated with the debt collection agency.

Evangeline took the stairs with weary steps and made her way to the first floor of the hospital wing in the east section of the vast building. A dull quiet damped the ward like a shroud, although there was never complete silence - a cough, a shout, someone wailing, someone kicking off through their drug-dulled senses - there was always something amiss. Coat removed and hung in her locker, she boiled the kettle and made herself a cup of tea in the nurses' comfort room, then checked her watch; with eight minutes remaining before the start of her shift, she felt quite at ease sitting back on the comfortable chair and drinking her tea in peace—until her thoughts turned to the patient in Room 12.

Barry Putchinski, or the Fenland Ripper as he was infamously called, was a long-term inmate whose health had declined dramatically in the last year, and particularly the last month. Moved to the hospital wing after a fit three months ago, he now looked to be at death's door, and Evangeline was sure, particularly given the medicalised end-of-life pathway he had been put on yesterday, that Room 12 would be his last cell of residence.

In recent weeks, Evangeline had read Putchinski's biography with relish. Written by one of the other inmates, a horror author with a fascination for serial killers, it was a truly fascinating insight into the mind of a monster but which read, disconcertingly, as a eulogy. The author, still incarcerated in D Wing, was himself a criminally insane copycat killer 'specialising', as he rather proudly put it, 'in the work of Jeffrey Dahmer and Hannibal Lecter'. It had been pointed out to the author that Hannibal Lecter wasn't a real person, but he'd responded with disparagement that he knew he was real because he had 'often consulted him for advice'.

After reading the book, Room 12 held an especial horror for Evangeline, and she had knelt to pray that Seth Golding, the author, never became ill enough to warrant a bed in the hospital wing. A cold shiver ran down her spine as she drank the last dregs of tea and watched the seconds tick to eleven o'clock, marking the start of her night shift. Unable to put it off any longer, she made her way to the ward and went through the routine 'change over' with veteran nurse Betty Ramsden and Suzy Pollock's replacement, Jayne Seddon, then made her way to the first patient of the night, Barry Putchinski.

Peering through the mesh of wire reinforcing the glass panel in the door of Room 12, she scanned the space inside. It was empty apart from the hospital bed and its surrounding paraphernalia which was deliberately kept to a minimum. The entire room was white. Apart from being clinical, the colour allowed the nurses and security staff to see anything untoward like a hidden weapon or even a hidden inmate. On one memorable occasion, a patient with a grudge found his way past security and prematurely ended the life of another.

On the bed, in the middle of the room, wrists and ankles shackled to the bed, lay the emaciated figure of Barry Putchinski. The thick leather straps around his wrists, with their solid brass buckles, seemed like overkill, but Evangeline knew, as did the entire staff at HMP Portland, Prison for the Criminally Insane, that not one of the inmates could be trusted—ever.

Remembering the descriptions of Putchinski's 'work' so vividly described in Golding's unpublished glorification of his life, Evangeline unlocked the door and, swallowing to lubricate her drying mouth, entered the room.

"Water!" Putchinski's weak voice rose from the bed though it didn't seem to come from the man's emaciated throat.

Evangeline took the clipboard from the end of his bed, and gripped it whilst turning the papers; a flimsy barrier between herself and the evil that wafted from the man strapped to the bed. She swallowed again, her mouth even drier, but treated the patient with her usual kindness. "I'm sorry, Barry, but Doctor Raymond says no fluids."

"Kill me!" he rasped. "He wants to kill me."

"Now, now," she said with a surge of pity as the man's eyes moistened. "You've got your drip. That'll give you enough fluids to keep you going, it's just we don't want you choking. You gave us all a scare yesterday." She took a step closer to take the readings from the heartrate monitor permanently hooked to Barry's arm, thankful that she didn't have to touch his mottled and paper-thin skin.

"Water!"

Unable to stand the sight of his parched lips and tear-filled eyes, Evangeline soaked a sponge secured to a foot-long stick in fresh water and brushed his lips. "I shouldn't be doing this. Doctor Raymond said not to."

Barry grunted his thanks, sucked at the sponge, then coughed.

Evangeline regretted her kindness. "Don't you go choking on me!"

"More!" Barry grabbed for the sponge with his shackled hand.

"Just hold on," she replied before dipping the sponge into the water and holding it once more to his lips. "Steady!" she said as he sucked greedily.

Thirst quenched, he sank back into his pillow. Quiet seconds passed, the patient unmoving, until his rasping voice broke the silence. "Free!" His eyes glittered with excitement. He rattled his tied wrists. "Free!"

"You know I can't."

"Free!" he insisted, pulling at the chains, the effort at forming the word obvious.

Ignoring him, and attempting to shake off a waft of revulsion, she busied herself with the routine hourly observations she had to take for Barry and the other patients on the ward. As the night progressed, Barry's temperature dropped, along with his heartrate, until both were consistent with the final hours of life.

"Free," he repeated as Evangeline re-entered the room after taking note of another patient's vital signs.

"You know I can't undo them, Barry," she said with a weary sigh and glanced at the leather straps as she closed the door. An edgy laugh from the emaciated prisoner made her skin crawl.

"Yes! Free!" His sandpaper voice wheedled through missing teeth. "Barbara ... Noelle ... Mary ... Doretta ..." Each name burst from dry lips like torn paper.

"That's enough, Barry!" she chided, recognising the names of his victims.

Ignoring her, he cackled then continued. "Annie ... Betty ... Doris ..." He squealed with delight. "Eve ... Eve ... Eve ...." The heartrate monitor beeped, and his shackled wrists shook violently against the bed as he forced himself to sit. "Eee ... van ...

je ... leen!" he screamed. The tendons of his neck were taut like wire about to snap.

Stepping back in horror, Evangeline watched as he bucked against his shackles, screaming her name with a voice grating like chalk on a board. With a slump, he fell back on the bed, and took one final, enormous gasp. The heart monitor flatlined with a continual and monotonous whine.

"Holy mother of God!" Evangeline crossed herself and continued to stare at the prone body; half-hidden by stark white bedsheets, it was little more than a skeleton. As she took a tentative step forward to look at his contorted face, she held back a scream of fright as his hand dropped through the bars. The metal of his restraints clinked against the metal of the bed. A growing fog manifested over the body, shifting in the moonlight that seeped through the window. Standing in disbelief as it eddied and sparkled, the temperature in the room suddenly dropped. Evangeline's white breath billowed and danced with the fog as the hairs on her arm stood on end. Goose bumps rose on her flesh. Clutching the clipboard to her chest, knees trembling, she watched as the fog lifted, took shape, and rose as a human form to the ceiling. Cold sweat beaded on her forehead as dark and hollow eyes stared down, and she realised with horror that she was witnessing the departing soul of Barry Putchinski.

She scanned the floor, expecting a black hole filled with demons to open up, their grasping talons ready to take Barry to the burning chasm of hell, or at least a super-heated purgatorial waiting room. Seeing nothing, she quickly checked the ceiling for a tunnel, or a bright and shining light. Again, nothing.

Realising she was alone with the evil and unfettered being that was Barry Putchinski's soul, a bead of sweat dribbled at her temple, and she took a step towards the door. Black hollows followed her retreat and, as she reached for the door's handle, the apparition contorted its mouth to shout a silent 'Free!' before melting through the closed window and disappearing into the dark November night.

CHAPTER ONE

Fourteen Years Later, Thornton Abbey

The first clue Frankie D'Angelo had that the 'ghost' the crew of 'Ghost Hunter PI' had just captured on video wasn't real, was the floury footprints in the grass across the abbey's lawn. What the crew were doing had become blatantly obvious, and she berated herself for being so slow to realise the tricks they were playing. She wanted so badly to believe that the show she was filming, was contracted to work on for another eight months, was a serious outfit looking for real ghosts. She had been wrong. Spectacularly wrong.

Speaking from the mobile studio parked on the grass beside the ladies' toilet block at the edge of the abbey's gardens, Dean's voice was tinny in her ear. "It's as clear as day, Frankie!" He continued jabbering as she processed what she had just seen. "You can see a clear outline of the apparition. It's energy is very strong. Did you see it?"

The earpiece squealed in her ear as Keith, the cameraman, shifted the camera on his shoulder—apparently the small movements added to viewer excitement, making the film appear as found footage. "Nope!"

Silence, and then, "Well at least the viewers saw it. Callum, did you see it?"

"I felt its energy, Dean," Callum replied from his position at the abbey's stone archway.

"It ran past me, Dean," Jake added, his voice heard through the communal communications network. "I felt the brush of cold as it passed."

They're all in on it! Realising that she was probably the only member of the crew who wasn't in on the deceit, embarrassment pricked Frankie's cheeks. A ghostly white apparition ran in the distance, and Frankie had followed at a sprint, narrating the chase with Keith barely keeping up. Unseen by the viewer, and ignored by the camera, footprints with a sprinkling of white powder were obvious across the damp grass. A former theatre actress, Frankie suspected that the powder was the same substance used by the props department, aka Melody Singer, to create the ghost of Hamlet's father in her last production.

The provincial critics had loved her version of Ophelia, fawning over the thinness and paper-white skin that had given her portrayal an ethereal, unhinged, quality. What they didn't know was that Frankie was terribly ill, unable to eat, and on the verge of a breakdown. Working with that particular director, Edward Brooke, and the truculent, egotistical Terrence Lording who played Hamlet, set off stress so bad that she would hallucinate on stage and was eventually forced to 'retire' from the show. After one particularly difficult between-show rehearsal - there had been multiple confrontations between herself and Lording, as well as intense bickering between Lording and the director – a mutilated figure appeared in the front stalls and she had collapsed.

The unsympathetic director had looked at her with scorn as she'd explained the reason for resigning from the play due to have its first West End performance the following Wednesday. He had shouted at her to pull herself together and, being deeply superstitious, screamed that she would 'never work again' on one of his stages if she breathed 'a word of this nonsense'.

Getting the host job on 'Ghost Hunter PI' was a step down from the West End, but it was at least work, paid more and, for the most part, the crew were a good laugh. The hallucinations disappeared, her grip on reality returned to normal, and the 'sightings' were also witnessed by the crew and caught on camera, therefore proving that she wasn't going mad.

For Frankie, the revelation that they had tampered with the ghost hunting equipment was more devastating than the lies. The equipment showed multiple readings, proof of ghostly activity, and the readings were always followed by a sighting that was generally caught on camera. During filming Frankie saw numerous 'ghosts' that weren't caught on camera nor mentioned by the team. She presumed these 'unseen' apparitions were the cause of the equipment's intense readings but, if they were all faked, it meant she was hallucinating again and - her head began to throb - that meant there was something wrong with her, some mental illness. The word schizophrenia hovered in her mind.

Her fellow host turned to camera and addressed the audience, finishing with, "Join us tomorrow as we delve into just who the ghost that haunts Thornton Abbey really is."

As soon as Dean called 'cut', she pulled the earpiece from her ear and was violently sick off camera. None of the crew came to her aide.

The following morning, back at Dean's office, Frankie argued, "But it's all rubbish! We're just leading people on."

"That's television for you. No one says it has to be real."

"But that's how you're selling it!"

Dean, the show's executive producer, script writer, director, and often cameraman, made an exaggerated and patronising sigh as though talking to a difficult child. "Listen, it's all part of the plot—like a literary hoax. The show is a fake, of course, sure, but Callum swore he'd seen a ghost in a churchyard at his interview, and Jake described experiencing multiple sightings from being a teenager, so I parked my disbelief and went along with it for the first week. I was stupid enough to think that we'd got some real psychics on board, but it turns out Callum was lying and Jake has a mild form of schizophrenia."

Frankie sensed Dean's lies, swallowed as a rush of cold passed over her, then asked, "And Jake's still working?"

"Yes, he's a functioning schizophrenic. His doctors have confirmed it, and we can't just fire people because they're loop-… I mean, struggling with their mental health; there are laws these days. Listen. To be honest, all the ghost stuff is … well it's just not real. We're making entertainment. People want to believe, so we'll give them what they want. Me—I've never seen a ghost in my life and never will; they just don't exist. At the end of the day, I gave the contracted psychics, ghost whisperers, whatever you want to call them, the benefit of the doubt, but they were fakes, and I still had a show to deliver. It would have bankrupt me not to pull it off."

"Between a rock and a hard place then," she offered, taking the path of least resistance.

His eyes brightened. "Exactly. There, you see. I knew you'd understand. But you knew it all along anyway, didn't you," he stated. "You don't really believe in ghosts, do you? Not really?"

She rolled her eyes in an 'as if!' gesture, then forced a smile. "Of course not."

"Listen, I'm sorry for not letting you in on it all, but we needed your honest reaction—it makes much better television that way; like John Hurt in 'Alien'. Did you know that the actors had no idea what was about to happen when the alien burst from his rib cage?"

She shook her head; science fiction wasn't her thing.

"Well, the director, Ridley Scott, set them all up and it was worth it; their reactions are stunning. You should watch it some time."

She made a noncommittal nod and her mind churned back to yesterday. At home, last night, she'd realised that the clues were there, that the ghosts the show 'found' were all part of the script. Dean had just been clever at planting the evidence without her noticing, and what the cameras showed in the final cut had all been manipulated via production software. She couldn't admit that a large part of her had ignored the evidence of his deceit. She so desperately wanted to believe they'd really find a ghost; it would be proof that she wasn't going mad, and that the ethereal figures that had drifted past her in school, or sat behind her on the bus to college, or rose into the air from the crashed lorry on her first day of work, were real. An ache began to throb at the base of her skull; but if there were no ghosts then - she could barely whisper the words, even to herself – then perhaps she was a 'functioning schizophrenic', just like Jake.

Yeah! You're batshit crazy.

Tension tightened across her chest. Adrenalin coursed through her veins, and her hands trembled.

A loony, just like Jake.

Thoughts continued to churn as her head throbbed.

Dean will get rid of you, if he finds out!

She yelped as a sudden stab of pain seared her temple.

"Frankie!" Dean asked with a worried frown.

The edges of her vision began to dull and darken, and she swayed as her legs became unsteady. A chill brushed her skin. Dean reached to steady her. Reality seemed to be fading.

"Frankie?"

Thankful of Dean's grip on her elbow, she leant into him, and closed her eyes in an effort to alleviate the pain in her head.

"Sit down."

Following his instructions, she allowed him to lead her to the sofa. She opened her eyes to another stab of pain and a grey shadow filling the corner on the far side of the room. Flashing lights bounced around the contours of Dean's body.

"Are you alright?" he asked as she screwed her eyes tight shut.

Just seeing things that don't exist! Nausea swelled in her belly. "Yes, just a migraine coming on, I think." She fumbled for the packet of migraine medication permanently carried in her bag, and dry-swallowed two pills. Dean offered her a sip of his bottled water. She took it gladly as he continued to hover.

Her head buzzed.

The grey man stood stock still in the corner.

Damn! ... Just ignore it. He's not real, stupid! You're just a schizo, Frankie! Same as Jake. Head in hand, eyes tight shut, she stifled a groan.

"Can I get you anything else? Do you need a doctor?"

"No, thanks. You've helped enough. It's just a migraine." The hairs on her neck and arms stood on end as the cold in the room deepened. Dean shivered.

"By heck! That air-con is sharp today." Walking to the far corner, where the grey shape stood, Dean gave a theatrical 'Br-rr!' and poked at the control panel. "That should do it."

Overwhelmed by the need to get out of the room and into the sunlight, Frankie thanked Dean for his help and, ignoring his suggestion that she sit for a while, stood to leave.

The grey shape stepped out of the corner.

Breath caught in Frankie's throat. She turned from the hazy figure, and focused on the door. *It's not real. It's not real. You're just stressed. Stay calm.*

"Eight pm!" Dean called as she stepped into the hallway.

The figure stood at his shoulder.

"Be on location at the abbey by eight."

The door swung shut and she staggered down the stairs of Dean's trendy harbour-side office and out to the carpark. Glad of the daylight, but with trembling hands and a still nauseated belly, she located her car and crossed the tarmac at a run, slumping into the seat with relief, berating herself for being spooked by her own imagination; the grey shadow wasn't real and, like the purple haze and dancing lights around Dean, it was just a symptom of the migraine brought on by stress. *It had seemed so real though!* Goosebumps had even risen along her arm with the cold. *Don't be stupid, Frankie! It's just your imagination; the air conditioning cycled to chilly—that's all.* She took a large breath to relieve the tension across her shoulders and started the car. With the headache reduced, and the flashing lights nowhere to be seen, she mused on how quickly the medication had worked this time, and her thoughts turned to the bottle of wine at home. As she left the carpark, she swallowed another pill.

CHAPTER TWO

Hemlock House

Kathy Fielding ran a finger along the dado rail of the wide hallway, rubbing the dust between her fingers, and making a mental note to ask Alicia, the House Keeper to arrange the cleaning of the woodwork, including all picture rails, panelling, skirting, and doors. Keeping Hemlock House to the standard expected by its residents was a continual cycle of cleaning, polishing, dusting, and washing, but the retreat was exclusive, the cost of staying high, and the standards expected by the guests and the retreat's owner, nothing less than immaculate. All this, including dealing with new guests, and making sure their stay was as stress-free as possible, was Kathy's responsibility.

Upstairs, there was no evidence of the banging that had woken her from a deep sleep for the fourth night in a row; several thuds from somewhere in the house had been followed by an eerie wail but, in her half-conscious state, she had fallen back to sleep and now retained only a vague awareness that the event occurred, deciding that it must be part of a recurring dream. Apart from the clinking of breakfast plates and glasses being removed from the dining room by the household staff, the house had a quiet placidity, just how she, and its troubled guests, liked it. Taking the final step down the wide staircase into the spacious entrance hall, she breathed a sigh of contentment. Pink-frilled peonies cut from the greenhouse, and arranged in an antique blue and white Chinese vase on the circular table at the hallway's centre, were stunning in the bright morning light.

A vibration in her pocket alerted her to an incoming call and she quickly stepped into the privacy of her office. The mobile's screen read, 'Margaret Beulieu', and Kathy experienced a slight throb at the back of her head. The caller was the demanding and particularly influential agent of Marcy Devereux, a middle-aged television star due to start a new, and very lucrative, contract working on a soap at the end of the month. She was also showing the classic signs of burnout accompanied by a crushing anxiety. Margaret, the agent, had contacted the retreat's owner, had the necessary non-disclosure and privacy agreements signed within forty-five minutes and returned via email, and booked Marcy in for a two-week stay before the commencement of filming on the Costa Blanca in Spain. Together with regular therapy sessions with their resident psychologist, she was also to undergo a series of beauty and spa therapies, alongside a detoxification programme. All of this was in accordance with the retreat's holistic, whole-body approach to healing, as well as to ensure that she was in peak condition at the start of filming.

As the conversation ended, a tension headache took grip at the back of Kathy's head. Marcy had called the agent in the middle of the night in absolute terror, convinced that 'something' was in her room. Margaret, a brusque, no-nonsense woman, explained that she had placated the troubled actress by suggesting that the vision was just part of a nightmare she had woken from. She had then questioned whether Marcy really was going through a detox, or 'somehow' had access to alcohol. Kathy had bridled at the unspoken accusation that one of her staff was supplying Marcy with the forbidden beverage, but managed to maintain a professional façade during the conversation. She replaced the mobile into the pocket of her tailored trousers and checked her appearance in the large mirror above the fireplace. A neatly proportioned redhead with a pretty face and shoulder-length curling hair, dressed in a closely fitted, and immaculately ironed, white shirt, stared back. Adjusting her hair, Kathy smiled at her reflection in an effort to enable a sense of peacefulness to return - a trick she'd learnt from the retreat's owner - but was startled by a flicker in the mirror. Swinging to the movement, she found nothing. "Silly woman!" She whispered. "It's just the light." Turning once more to the mirror, she took comfort from dappled sunlight dancing on the apple tree's leaves beyond the window. Then, taking a deep and calming breath, she followed the flow of exhalation with a sweep of her hands. With refreshed determination, she strode from her office to find Dr. Alexander Mansard, the retreat's resident psychologist, to arrange a 'conversation' between himself and Marcy Devereaux.

CHAPTER THREE

Office of Marshall & Blaylock Investigations

As Peter Marshall placed the receiver back in its cradle and made a mental note to tell Meredith, his partner in Marshall & Blaylock Investigations, that they really needed a more specific name for their business, she walked through the door. A neat woman, with aquiline nose and piercing blue eyes, her hair was a perfectly coiffured halo of silver as she smiled her greeting. Make up understated as always, with just a hint of blush and lipstick, she appeared fresh and full of energy, and Peter was once again impressed by her vigour; at sixty-three years old, most women her age had given in to middle age spread and hobbled around on overwhelmed knees.

"Good morning, Peter! Such a beautiful day."

The energy that radiated off her this morning was intense, and Peter's own, querulous, slightly darker, energy was lifted. "It is, Meredith. I take it the meeting last night went well."

"Oh, Peter!" she exclaimed as she placed her large and well-weathered briefcase on the desk. "It did."

"He turned up then?"

"Yes!" The joy in her eyes was obvious and she began an animated recital of the previous evening. Last week they had been called in to help a recently bereaved and desperate widow who believed her house had become haunted. It was the typical scenario: banging doors, cold spots, things appearing where they hadn't been before.

"And he went willingly?"

"Yes! It was ... emotional. The widow was beside herself until she understood why her husband hadn't passed on to the other side."

"Which was?"

"Oh, also typical in these cases. His love for her was holding him back, and he just wanted to continue protecting her as he had done throughout their marriage."

Peter nodded. They'd had several similar cases, although some were easier to resolve than others, depending on a) the level of intelligence of the 'dearly departed' and b) whether their continued presence in the home was due to a genuine desire to protect their widowed wife, or to control her. In the latter it was far more difficult to rid the widow of their newly dead spouse; the tentacles of jealousy could be strong and held their grasp beyond the grave. In those cases, the resistance to finally letting go was difficult to break. At this point, it would often take a man-to-man talk to resolve the situation, and Peter was proud to acknowledge that, so far, he had a one hundred percent success rate in these matters.

"Once I explained to George, that was the husband's name, that Bea had friends and family, as well as their own two adult sons who dote on their mother, to help her through the years until she was ready to join him on the other side, he said his goodbyes and left. Poor Bea was upset, but we had a cup of tea and then cleansed the house together, and by the time I left she was at peace, as is George." Meredith sighed with satisfaction.

"And she's paid the bill?"

"Ah, I have no doubt that she will. The first instalment was paid promptly and I'm sending out the final invoice today."

"Good." Peter didn't like to be stern about the payment for services, but Meredith, despite her very organised and business-like attitude, was also extremely empathic, and polite, and didn't like to push when a client was slow to pay. This was another area that Peter excelled in, particularly as neither of them could live on thin air, and the proceeds from their investigations were an important source of income.

He remembered the earlier phone call. "Meredith, I think that perhaps we should have a more specific name for our business. I've already had two calls this morning from people wanting to set honey traps."

Meredith laughed as she walked through to the kitchenette, the only other room in their 'office', apart from the toilet which she steadfastly refused to use. "Perhaps then, we should branch out and offer our services to suspicious spouses?"

Peter knew she was joking. "Seriously though, how about Marshall and Blaylock Psychic Investigations?"

The kettle began to boil and Meredith stepped out of the kitchenette to reply. "My only fear, Peter, is that if we proclaim our services in that way, then we would have all kind of ... I hesitate to call them this, perhaps unhinged is a kinder word ..."

"Nutters?"

"Yes, all kind of ... nutters, and hoaxers, calling us."

"Well, perhaps we can get a receptionist? Someone to share the responsibility and maybe even do the invoicing?"

"Money, Peter. We just don't have enough to pay anyone else."

As he mulled over her response, understanding her point, but also tired of the continual irrelevant enquiries, the telephone rang. He raised his brows in a 'here's another one' gesture and answered the phone. Relieved when the caller asked if he could help with 'ghosts', and explained quite why they need his help, Peter relaxed and gave Meredith a thumbs up. Kitchenette door closed to block out the noise of the boiling kettle, she sat in her chair, listening to the conversation.

CHAPTER FOUR

Hemlock House

A lowering sun cast long shadows along the hallway as Kathy watched Marcy Devereux leave Dr. Mansard's office. She waited until the woman had stepped into the dining room before making her approach. A quiet knock at the door was answered by 'enter'. Entering the room, Kathy closed the door softly behind her, and sat in the large armchair beside the open fire. She allowed herself to sink into the soft leather, making her best effort to appear calm and collected despite the unease which had shifted over her in the last hour as the light began to fade.

"I've always loved this room," she said as Dr. Mansard moved away from his office chair and joined her beside the fire, relaxing into an equally large armchair of dark green velvet. Newly lit, the kindling crackled and spat, and tightly scrunched balls of newspaper burned with green, then yellow, then orange flames. "It has such a comforting feel about it."

"The whole house is magnificent, Mrs Fielding-"

"Kathy, Doctor Mansard. Please—call me Kathy."

"Well, then I insist that you call me Alexander ... Kathy." Crow's feet wrinkled around bright green eyes that were without definition to the outer iris. She shifted her gaze to the hearth. Alexander added another log to the newly burning fire.

"The house *is* magnificent. It was so run down in the beginning. Mrs Maybank put in a huge amount of work to restore it." Kathy remembered the fraught months of dealing with builders, plumbers, electricians, and decorators, and then the weeks of 'cleansing' that followed.

"And worked even harder to build her reputation."

"Yes." Mesmerised by the flames, memories of the past years flickered in her mind: the renovation of the property from dilapidated wreck, the first 'client' booked in before the first room was properly finished, the desperate rush to furnish the room before they arrived. Their struggle to launch the business had been Herculean, but they had worked together, put in the hours, and by the second year were in profit, and could even afford to pay themselves a living wage. Their reputation had grown, along with the profit, and now, ten years later, the business was thriving.

"But you haven't come here to exchange pleasantries about the décor, Kathy."

"No, obviously." She returned to a more business-like attitude. "Marcy Devereux. She's now demanding that she be given another suite. How best are we to help her?"

"Marcy and I spoke at length about her experiences over the last few nights. I think that her request to move is down to me."

Kathy raised a brow. "I thought it was only last night that she'd had a nightmare?"

"She complained of feeling terribly anxious over the last few days-"

"And has she had access to alcohol?"

Alexander raised an eyebrow this time.

Kathy regretted her interruption and the push for information.

"She was at pains to tell me that she has been sober for six years, and I do believe her."

"She complained to her manager that she felt there was someone in her room."

"Marcy is suffering from extreme levels of anxiety which I believe are intimately linked to her concerns about ageing in an industry obsessed by youth. She feels certain that her new contract will be cut short, or that she'll be side-lined by a younger actress."

Kathy nodded. "In their business, it *is* a real concern."

"True, but Marcy isn't ready to accept that, and experiences massive anxiety at the thought of not being considered for roles. She is also obsessed with worry about her appearance on the screen. She mentioned the cruelty of HD television numerous times during our conversation."

"She's afraid of negative public opinion and being without work, then."

"Yes."

"And you think that the anxiety is linked to her ... hallucinations?"

"I'm not convinced that she has experienced auditory or visual hallucinations. I'm more inclined to believe that the noises and voices-"

"Voices?"

"Yes, she claims to have heard a voice reciting words she can't decipher."

"Are you sure she hasn't been drinking? Or, perhaps ... drugs?"

"Well, it is possible, obviously, but she's adamant that is not the case. I think it more likely that she is experiencing night terrors. It can be hard to discern between the unconscious and waking state at times."

"She has certainly made enough noise!"

"She's a woman desperate for attention. This environment, despite all the therapies and beauty treatments, isn't the right place for a personality such as Marcy Devereux; her ego is too fragile."

"But that's exactly what we cater to, and she gets attention almost twenty-four hours a day here!"

"She is attended to, that's true, but she isn't holding court."

"Not the centre of attention then?"

"Exactly. The night terrors have given her the perfect excuse, one she thinks is justified in drawing attention to herself. Or it could be the case that the nightmares are playing on her mind, which, in her fragile state, she has interpreted as a threat, and the barrier that separates reality and fantasy has been thinned to a point where she's not sure if what she is hearing is real or just a dream.

"So, in short, she had a nightmare from which she awoke thinking the dream was her reality."

Alexander nodded.

"And then she exaggerated her fear in order to gain the attention she needs."

"Yes, rather like a naughty child acting up to get the attention of a neglectful parent."

"We haven't neglected Marcy!"

"No, absolutely not. She has a highly detailed and thorough programme written up for her, I've read her file. What it lacks is the excitement she craves."

Kathy shook her head; she would never understand these 'creative' types. With Evangeline, she had created a virtual paradise where they could have their meltdowns in absolute privacy, yet they still wanted more.

"What do you suggest I do, Alexander? Another night like last night could cause all sorts of problems, not only in disturbing the peace of the other residents, but her agent is particularly influential among the celebrity set, one wrong word from her, and the business will suffer."

Alexander stoked the fire, prodding at the flames with an iron poker. "Assure her that there is nothing to worry about. Move her to another room, and encourage her to take a warm and relaxing bath before bedtime."

"That's it?"

"I've spoken to her; she was far calmer when she left than when she arrived. I'm sure a new suite will break the psychological link she has between her nightmare and the bedroom. Perhaps a calmative before bedtime?"

"She could have a bedtime drink of hot chocolate, or Ovaltine; we don't offer anything stronger here."

"Sounds perfect."

CHAPTER FIVE

Providence House, 6:30 pm

As Kathy returned to her office, only mildly reassured about Marcy Devereux, Frankie left her apartment with unease and a growing sense of foreboding, but also relieved to leave her home where, throughout the afternoon, flickers of movement had plagued her peripheral vision. However, the climbing anxiety about facing the crew and going through another night of pretend ghost hunting at Thornton Abbey, with the possibility that she would lose her mind on camera and descend into some sort of hideous psychotic break, was worse.

"None of it is real," she whispered as she stepped over the threshold and into the building's wide hallway.

Built for a wealthy merchant in the mid-nineteenth century the once grand family residence still retained its high ceilings, ornate plasterwork cornices and coving, and shuttered sash windows. She could almost hear the rustle of crinoline and gentlewomen's laughter, and the scurrying of their work-worn maids, along the corridor. A musty smell pervaded the space which she put down to the old carpet warmed by the afternoon's sun, and perhaps the damp behind the inch-thick skirting boards original to the mid-Victorian house.

A flash in her imagination of Dean, Callum, and Jake waiting for her beside the trailer at Thornton Abbey tightened her chest and she took a breath. "Hold it together, D'Angelo. You're a professional." She dry-swallowed as she pulled the door to a close. Aware of speaking aloud, she quickly checked the corridor for neighbours who might overhear her mutterings. Relieved that the space was empty, she continued. "You can fall apart tomorrow, after a perfectly filmed night of ghost hunting."

She attempted a small laugh - her predicament was risible - but the laugh stuck in her throat and grew to a sob; the hallucination at Dean's office that morning had been deeply unsettling, and she had made her way home, racing at the edge of the speed limit, desperate to fling herself into the softness of her bed and close her eyes to the greyed-out man that had stood at his shoulder. However, after only half an hour back in her flat, she had felt the unnerving sensation of being watched. Scouring the flat, trying to pinpoint the movement, had proved futile, and she had finally, nervously, dismissed it as evidence of her increasing stress.

A search on the internet for 'symptoms of breakdown' had been unhelpful, but when she searched on 'symptoms of psychosis' and 'symptoms of schizophrenia' she had closed the web page, and then the browser, and broken down in tears. At the back of her mind a nagging voice told her she was being ridiculous, that googling your symptoms on the internet was dumb, and that diagnosing herself with a mental illness was just plain silly, but the knowledge that she had at least some symptoms of schizophrenia and psychosis played on her deepening anxiety with painful prods.

Despite the sense of unravelling, she had showered, forced herself to focus, and researched the history of the abbey to ensure that she had something interesting to say on camera when the time came; Dean's scripts were rather dry and contrived, and she had decided to rely on her flair for improvisation when the script seemed too fanciful or dull. Afterall, it wasn't just the programme's ratings that were at stake, as well as paying the rent, she was relying on its success to push her career to the next level.

The door to her apartment shut with a click and Frankie turned to make her way down the narrow servants' staircase, unaware of the small boy watching her leave. As she disappeared, he melted through the door, travelling back into her apartment.

The forty mile drive to Thornton Abbey was uneventful, and Frankie flipped through her CD collection as she travelled along the motorway, flicking with dissatisfaction from song to song, and album to album, until she finally settled on Credence Clearwater Revival's 'Greatest Hits', listening to the tracks, and her favourite, 'Bad Moon Rising', on a loop until she finally reached the abbey. Berating herself for not booking a room at a local hotel, and wondering if it was too late to make a reservation, she noticed, with a start, the familiar dark red Porsche of her agent, Sally Gibson-Stanley, parked beside Dean's gleaming black Range Rover. Sliding her own, nearly vintage, definitely battered, Volkswagen Polo into a space on the other side of the carpark, she joined Jake's non-descript Ford something, and Callum's rusting and flower-stickered Volkswagen campervan. Callum had taken great pride in telling her that his 'splitty' had been at the Weeley Festival, Britain's notoriously violent answer to Woodstock, twenty years before he had even been born. She'd peered inside to its shabby interior complete with tiny kitchen, and said, 'It's fantastic!' whilst hoping that the cushioned seats that doubled up as a mattress hadn't also been at Weeley.

Filled with the foreboding of a small child standing outside the headmaster's office, Frankie entered the office-cum-studio, and was greeted by three faces each offering a pitying, apprehensive, smile. Frankie's discomfort ratcheted another turn as she realised that Dean must have called her agent after the incident in his office that morning.

A professional eye appraised her in a flash before Sally's face quickly softened, "Frankie!"

"On time, good girl," Dean said as Frankie was lost in Sally's hug of greeting. Swinging back to the row of monitors, he spoke into a microphone, communicating with the cameraman. A ghostly figure dressed in medieval 'peasant' costume walked across the screen and Dean's smile broadened. "Perfect! Just bloody perfect". His voice was little more than a whisper and then, in a louder voice, and into the microphone, he said. "You've nailed it, Sandra. We'll be filming in ..." he checked his watch, "forty minutes. Take her back to the trailer. Thanks."

So, no more deceit. The lies are all out in the open. "Sandra?"

"Sandra McCoy. She used to work at the BBC in their makeup department. She's on maternity leave and needs some extra cash so we've got her for a couple of nights." Dean leant back in his chair with a broad smile still fixed across his face. "She wasn't cheap, but the ghost looks amazing. We'll even be able to get some close-ups this time." He held Frankie's gaze for a second, waiting for her reaction, then turned his attention back to the screens.

Sensing his judgement, she swallowed down her disapproval at deceiving the public, along with her unease at every nuance of her reaction being watched. *Be professional, Frankie.*

You need this job. "Which ... ghost ... is the actor meant to portray?"

Dean swivelled back, eyes glittering, his own disapproval at Frankie's lack-lustre reaction gone. "Well," he smiled, "my wife's research turned up some interesting history, it's on one of the information boards in the abbey grounds, but barely known." Frankie suppressed a sigh; if the story was on one of the information boards, then it was hardly 'barely known'. "A young woman became romantically entangled with one of the novice monks. Once the abbot discovered they were 'at it', they were both punished, but escaped, and tried to elope by rowing across the river." He gestured to the wide and swift-flowing, murky river less than three miles from the abbey. "But the weather was treacherous, and the girl drowned. The young monk was dragged from the river but died a week later. There have been sightings of the girl running through the grounds, as well as the couple on the river bank." He chuckled.

With a gentle squeeze around Frankie's shoulder, Sally said, "I'll be on set with you tonight, Frankie."

"There's no need, really."

Sally and Dean exchanged a quick glance.

"Really, I'm fine."

"There's no point in me hiding behind an excuse, Frankie ... Dean called me after the ... incident last night and this morning."

Dean stared back at his monitors.

"He was concerned about you, that's all."

"You seemed ill," Dean added without turning around.

For Sally to have travelled the eighty miles from her home to the location, Dean must have laid it on thick. "I appreciate you travelling all of this way, but I'm fine. Honestly."

"Well, just look on it as one friend checking in on another. Dean said you seemed unwell, I wanted to make sure that one of my 'charges' wasn't going to flake out on me." She laughed, making light of the situation. "I have a reputation to uphold."

It was true, they were friends, but Sally's reference to protecting her reputation held the real truth; she was fiercely protective of her standing as an agent in the community. Known as one of the best, she would fight tooth and nail to get her 'charges' the best deals in the industry, but it was also known that she gave prima donnas, and shoddy directors, short shrift. That she was here, checking in on Frankie, meant that she had serious concerns.

"I'm not going to 'flake out,'" Frankie laughed with humour she didn't feel.

A firmer squeeze across her shoulders. "I'm sure you'll be absolutely fine. By the way, I'm planning a surprise party for Carey's fiftieth, will you come?" Carey was Sally's far older partner, an actor who flirted with Hollywood, and one whose career she had taken on as a project to prove herself in the industry. Their falling into love had been a surprise for them both, but ten years later they still seemed as besotted as the day they'd first met. Carey's career had recently taken off in the States, and he was increasingly in demand.

"I wouldn't miss it," Frankie replied with relief. Whatever Sally thought of her, she was still her friend.

"You too, Dean, and bring Audrey."

"Love to, lovie."

The tension in the room lifted, and then became business-like as Dean passed a sheaf of paper across to Frankie. "Today's script."

She replied by holding up a rolled sheaf, and smiled. "Lines learned, although I hope it's okay to improvise … here and there; I've been doing some research too."

The relief across Sally's face was obvious as Dean nodded. "That will be absolutely marvellous, Frankie. I knew you'd come through."

CHAPTER SIX

Hemlock House

With the main light switched off, a warm glow spread from Kathy's bedside lamp as she sat at the dressing table wiping a moist cotton wool pad across her cheek. The cleansing toner tingled on her skin, bringing with it a refreshing relief and ridding her of the façade of immaculately presented, coiffured, and in control persona she wore each day. With all 'guests' safely in their rooms, all demands and requests fulfilled, and all doors locked, Kathy could finally relax. At her temple, grey streaked through rich auburn as she pulled the brush through her hair for a final time before slipping into bed. Resting back on her pillow, she allowed her body to relax, noticing the pain in her back and joints as her muscles adjusted to their new position, and pushed away thoughts of the arthritis that crippled her mother.

The novel from her reading pile already chosen, she put on her glasses and reached for a terrifying book she had tried, and failed, to read as a teenager; a dog-eared copy of Stephen King's 'The Shining'. An hour passed and with each page she was drawn further into King's world until finally the words blurred and her eyelids lowered. She woke with a jolt, focused, then read several more sentences. Sleep drew her and, despite forcing herself awake, she only managed another half sentence before slipping into an exhausted, dream-filled oblivion.

The clat of her book as it slipped to the floor several hours later jolted her awake, and she twisted to turn off the bedside light, freezing as the blurred figure of a woman wavered in the corner. She stifled a scream, and screwed her eyes tight shut whilst simultaneously pulling the duvet over her head and shrinking back into her pillow. Heart pounding, every cell of her body quivered with terror but, as the seconds passed, the only sound she could hear was the pulse pounding in her head and her own shallow breathing. As the air beneath the duvet became heated and stuffy, she slowly lowered the cover to peak into the room. There was no evidence of anyone, or any *thing*, in the bedroom. Minutes passed as she scanned, then rescanned, every crevice and corner until she was certain of being completely alone. Trembling, she made a hurried dash to switch on the main light then pulled on her dressing gown, tightening the belt about her waist, and turning up the collar against her neck.

"Damned book!" she whispered as she sat heavily on the bed. "You're a stupid fool, Katherine Louise Fielding." Retrieving the horror novel, she dropped it into the bin, then made her way to the kitchenette along the hallway to make herself a cup of tea and calm her nerves.

In the narrow room, she spooned Earl Grey leaves into a brightly patterned teapot and then cut a fresh slice of lemon as she waited for the kettle to boil. Outside, the storm, threatened earlier in the day, had risen to a gale, and the apple tree tapped against the window downstairs. She made a mental note to ask Marlon, the groundskeeper, to cut it back, then reached for the kettle as steam billowed from its spout. Startled by a sudden long and pain-filled wail, boiling water splashed onto the counter. The hair at the back of her neck stood with painful prickling as water dripped to the floor.

"What on earth!" she hissed.

Another wail.

The kettle trembled in her hand and she lowered it to the counter, bowels loosening.

Thud!

The bare pendant light swung overhead.

Thud!

Tea forgotten, she pulled her gown tighter, and stepped out into the hallway. The cry resumed, this time as a sob, immediately followed by a thud from the floor above. Kathy made a quick mental scan of the layout of the house; directly above was the *Grace Kelly* suite, the rooms that Marcy Devereux had moved into this afternoon. She sighed with irritation; if the noise continued, the troubled woman would wake the entire house and risk upsetting its fragile inhabitants even further. Reasoning that it must have been Marcy's night terrors that had woken her on the previous few nights, and spooked her into experiencing a waking nightmare tonight, she made another mental note to ensure that the list of questions on the initial application form be extended to asking prospective clients if they had a history of sleep-walking or night terrors. They could then be placed in a part of the house where their disturbances would be less of a nuisance. Perhaps it was even time to add soundproofing to some of the rooms. Eve would resist that though; her love of the house extended to keeping it in its period state, and adding a layer of acoustic board to the walls would damage the elaborate plasterwork and original skirtings.

With a swish of her satin robe, she made her way to the upper floor and Marcy's suite of rooms. The wail of a woman's voice returned as she reached the landing and was accompanied by another thud. Arriving outside the suite, she took hold of the door's knob, and twisted. The latch pulled back, and the door opened to a scene that made her blood rise.

Stark light filled the room, almost bleaching out the details, but what stood in startling relief on the expensively papered walls was a scrawled crimson print that looked to have been written, Kathy noted with anger, in felt tip. The room was silent, and Marcy lay deep in sleep, silken face mask pulled over her eyes, oblivious to Kathy stepping inside the room to check the walls. If the wallpaper was ruined, then Ms. Devereux would have a horrible, and very expensive, surprise when she received her final bill. She stepped up to the wall, traced a finger over the letters, hoping that a crimson residue transferred to her skin. The walls were cold, almost damp, but the crimson ink remained intact—*permanent marker!* She read the graffiti, which all appeared to be in different, slightly shaky, hands: Barbara, Noelle, Mary, Doretta, Annie, Betty, Doris, and—Marcy Devereux! Kathy hissed, recognising the distinctive, and elaborate signature of Marcy Devereux with its swirling script and flourish on the final 'x'. Her anger rose at the temerity of the woman 'signing' her name on the wall like a delinquent teenager! As she continued to stare at the handwriting, the paper grew to be mottled, marked by rings of damp, and covered in an old-fashioned pattern of pink rosebuds and tendrils of ivy.

Behind her, Marcy shifted in the bed and pulled off her eye-mask. "Mrs Fielding, is that you?" she asked with a questioning frown, and pulled the cord for the main light. The room instantly brightened, and the writing disappeared.

With no evidence of writing, or any kind of damage, Kathy was suddenly an intruder. "Oh!" She dry-swallowed. *Think!* "I

... Yes, I wanted to check on you tonight. I thought I heard you talking in your sleep, perhaps having a nightmare, so I came to check."

"Oh, that is sweet of you," Marcy replied with her saccharine insincerity. "But I'm perfectly fine."

"Yes." Kathy forced a smile, struggling to shake off the anger, and now confusion, of the past seconds. "I ... well, goodnight." She pulled the door to close as Marcy pulled the light cord and lay back down.

"Night."

Casting a quick glance at the now undamaged walls, Kathy shut the door with a soft thud, and leant back against the wall, pulling her dressing gown tight, heart tripping as she tried to process what she had just seen. *There was nothing on the wall! But the names had been clearly scrawled in red ink! You imagined it!* She caught a sob in her throat; *but it had seemed so real!* With rising horror that the scene was an hallucination, she hurried back to her bedroom.

CHAPTER SEVEN

Thornton Abbey

A flicker of red caught Frankie's attention as she readjusted her earpiece. She took another swig of coffee. Filming had been stop-start since nine o'clock when she and Callum had recorded the introductory pieces for tonight's instalment of 'Ghost Hunter PI'. Research completed over the past week and the 'secret' history of the abbey uncovered earlier in the day, despite her massive anxiety attack, had become extremely useful as she and Callum veered from Dean's script with a genuinely interesting conversation on camera. Dean declared himself 'stoked' by the footage.

In another twenty minutes her break would be over, and 'ghost hunting' was to resume with a sighting of the tragic medieval maiden. The lies uncovered, or rather, the 'ghosts' revealed, a massive weight had lifted from Frankie's shoulders; knowing that the 'sightings' were scripted and she didn't have to be on tenterhooks, or scared half to death, waiting for the ghost to appear, was a relief. Now, feeling strangely drawn out of the comfort of the mobile studio, she stood in the grounds of the abbey, with breath billowing white, and a thermal coffee cup in hand.

The moon was a full and gleaming orb, with only the faintest wisp of clouds to blot out the stars, and the ruins of the abbey's church sat in creamy-grey relief against the dark grass. The massive gatehouse walls towered behind her.

Cold bit at Frankie's cheeks as the night began to echo with raised and shouting voices. The words were muffled, but a woman's rage and a man's anger were clear. Metal clanked. A door slammed, then footsteps pounded up wooden steps. Another door slammed shut. Searching the area, Frankie saw nothing. The shouting stopped, and she took another sip of coffee, whilst wondering who could be arguing. Footsteps crunched across the gravel immediately behind her. Startled, hot liquid from the thermal mug scalded her lips. The coffee mug slipped from her fingers with a clatter on the stones, and she turned to a young woman with a red beret. Face deathly pale in the moonlight, her eyes were black hollows, her lips a shining and ruby-red. Running past Frankie, close enough to touch, the woman disappeared into the shadows of the massive walls. Moments later she reappeared climbing the steps. A quick glance at the caretaker's lodge showed the door ajar and the lights on. Perhaps the source of the argument? In her walking boots, warm hat, and fleece, the woman must, Frankie reasoned, be part of the caretaking team that worked for English Heritage. She stooped to retrieve her coffee mug.

In the near distance, the convincing tones of Jake's near-baritone drifted from behind the church ruins as the woman climbed to the upper walkway along the top edge of the wall. If the noise had been picked up by the microphones, Dean would be fuming, or rubbing his hands in glee at the disturbance caught on film. Frankie drained the last of the coffee, expecting the woman to disappear through the door leading into the upper gatehouse. Instead, she turned from the doorway and climbed onto the wall's topping stones. They wobbled as she placed her boot on the edge.

With a sinking in her gut, Frankie shouted "Hey!" On the other side of the wall was a huge, probably fatal drop to the abbey's car park.

The woman seemed to lose her balance, but quickly righted herself.

"Hey! Come down."

With a flash of white to Frankie's left, Sally, wrapped in her white pashmina, stepped out of the caretaker's door. Behind her was the familiar figure of Neil Carson, the caretaker Frankie had met on their first arrival.

"A woman!" Frankie shouted at Sally then jabbed a finger at the top of the three-storey gatehouse. "She's on the wall!"

Sally broke into a run.

"I think she's going to jump!"

The woman turned unsteadily to face into the abbey.

"Don't!" Frankie screamed.

Sally's hand grasped Frankie's shoulder. "What is it?"

Frankie flinched at the touch, and continued to jab towards the top of the wall. "Someone, get her down!"

"Where is she, Frankie?" Sally scoured the walls for the woman.

"There!" Frankie jabbed her finger at the unsteady woman, her heart tripping. "She's going to jump!"

As Frankie broke free of Sally's grip, sprinting towards the stone steps, the woman on the wall, underlit by the solar lamps marking the walkway, made a pirouette and, arms akimbo, leant out over the precipice. In the next second, gravity pulled her down, and she fell into the dark.

"No!"

"Frankie, whatever is it?"

"The woman ... she jumped!" Turning from the steps, Frankie ran to the gates and through to the carpark. Sally and Neil followed.

"Frankie! Slow down. I didn't see a woman."

"What did she look like?"

"Call an ambulance!"

"What did she look like?"

Breathless, illuminating the base of the wall with the bright torch from her mobile phone, Frankie described the woman. "She was wearing a red beret, walking boots ... a ... an oversized fleece. Bright red lipstick."

Neil's face contorted to an ugly frown. "Colour of hair?"

"Blonde, I think. And curling. Her lips were bright red."

His lips thinned and, with an angry scowl, Neil grabbed Frankie's shoulder. "Is this some kind of joke?" Grip tightening, she buckled under the pain. "What the hell do you think you're doing?"

"You're hurting me!"

His fingers continued to dig into muscle. "Is that what this farrago is all about? Huh?"

"Get off!"

Releasing steel fingers digging into her shoulder, he turned to Sally. "Is it?"

Sally stared back with incomprehension.

"Is it?" The anger in Neil's voice was unmistakable, but it carried an undertone of pain.

"Neil, I don't understand-"

"The woman she just described ... it was Jill, my wife."

"Oh, my God! I ... call the police," Frankie urged. "She must be hurt!"

"I didn't see a woman, Frankie." Sally's expression hardened. "Neil, I have no idea-"

"My wife died two years ago." His words were clipped, the emotion bitten back. "She threw herself from the wall ..." He jabbed a finger at the top of the wall where the woman had stood. "From there."

Bright lights began to flash at the periphery of Frankie's vision.

Neil turned back to Frankie. "So ... so, you think you can come here and ... and claim to see the ghost of my wife and ..." He choked back tears. "And make ... make her death into entertainment!"

"Frankie! You didn't ... did you? Surely this isn't the improvisation you mentioned earlier?"

"No!" Frankie flinched from the pain in Neil's eyes. Sally's accusation was a punch to the gut. "Sally! You don't really think that I-"

"Neil, I must apologise on Frankie's behalf, but please understand that I had nothing to do with it," Sally added quickly.

Neil continued to stare at Frankie.

Heart racing, she replied, "I had no idea she was your wife ..."

"You disgust me!"

"... I just saw a woman walk up the stairs and then ... then throw herself from the ..." Unable to finish the sentence as white noise filled her ears, Frankie became unsteady and swayed. Bright lights flashing around the figures of Neil and Sally, broadened to fill her vision. Nausea swelled, and the last thing she heard before the blinding light turned to black, was her name being called.

CHAPTER EIGHT

Hemlock House

As Frankie was helped to the caravan that served as the crew's comfort room, Kathy Fielding drifted back to a fitful sleep where she dreamt of scrubbing at the names scrawled on the bedroom wall to the background of wailing voices.

The night passed without further incident and Kathy woke to the scratching of the apple tree on the window beneath her own and the thin sunlight of morning seeping through her curtains.

Barbara ... Noelle ... Mary ... Doretta ... Annie ... Betty ... Doris ... Marcy

The names rose in Kathy's memory, flooding her senses. *Barbara ... Noelle ...* Throwing back the covers she headed straight for the bathroom and showered, standing beneath the steaming water, shampooing her hair with fingernails that dug at her scalp, soaping her body with rapid strokes in an effort to remove the sensation of dread. The hallucination in her bedroom had been terrifying, as had the noises coming from Marcy's bedroom, but more terrifying was the realisation that none of it had been real, it was all the product of her imagination. Like the guests, she was losing her mind! Kathy's hands trembled as she combed through wet hair, dried it, then dressed. Before she reached the bottom of the grand staircase, still unable to calm her nerves, she determined to call the owner and ask for a leave of absence; if she were going mad, then she couldn't be responsible for Hemlock House and its guests.

Dr. Mansard attempted to catch her attention as she entered her office. She returned his call with a quick 'good morning' and 'I'll be with you in a minute' then locked the door and slumped into her chair. Her mind continued to churn, repeating the women's names, re-living the scenes in her bedroom, and in Marcy's. They had seemed so real, but there was just no way that they could be. She dialled the number, attempting to gather her fractured thoughts, before speaking to Eve.

The phone connected. "Kathy? It's very early ... is everything alright?"

Perceptive as ever. "Yes ... No! Oh, Eve ... I think I'm having a breakdown ..." Her words were met with silence on the other end as Eve gave her time to continue, the words that followed erupted as a stifled sob.

"Whatever is the matter, Kathy? This is so unlike you. I can hear that you're crying ... I shall wait for you to calm yourself and speak."

Seconds passed as Kathy took a breath to calm the chaotic emotion gripping her. She breathed through her mouth, easing the tension. "Last night ... I had an hallucination."

"Oh? Please ... go on."

For the next few minutes, all efforts at maintaining her professional demeanour gone, Kathy relived the night as her gentle friend listened. "It was horrendous, Eve. The thing in my room ... I swear it was there, but of course ... oh, my mind is breaking ..."

"Kathy, please, be calm. Sometimes we can ... see things that others can't."

"No, no. It was my own fault. I'd been reading a horror novel ... and you know that I really shouldn't read those!"

Eve's soft laugh brought a smile to Kathy's face; talking to Eve always soothed her often fractious nerves. "Well, you do have a very active imagination, Kathy. Perhaps you're right, perhaps it was triggered by the book. Which one was it?"

"*The Shining*."

"Now, that is one book even I can't read!"

Kathy laughed. "Oh, Eve, I knew talking to you would make me feel better, but I really ... perhaps I do need a break though. I actually went into Marcy Devereux's bedroom to investigate the noise and had some sort of hallucination whilst there. She woke up to find me in her room. What's worse is that the names that were on the wall keep repeating in my mind ... over and over!" She sighed with tension.

"Names?"

"Yes, they were scrawled all over the wall. I thought, at first, that they were actually on the wall, but as soon as Marcy woke, the spell broke and they disappeared. They're the same names I heard in my sleep, and now that I'm awake, they keep repeating."

"Can you tell me the names?"

"Yes, they're so clear! ... Barbara, Noelle, Mary, Doretta, Annie ... Betty, oh yes, and Doris, then Marcy." Eve didn't reply. Kathy continued. "They're so old-fashioned aren't they." Eve remained silent. "Eve ... are you there?"

When Eve spoke, her voice had taken a sombre tone. "Kathy, I don't want you to worry, but I'll be with you this afternoon."

"I'm sure that's not necessary, Eve! I know how important it is for you to be with Mister Saddler at the moment."

"George passed this morning. I'll go home and shower, and then be with you."

The line went dead with an uncharacteristically brusque click which only added to Kathy's tension; she had managed to upset Eve now!

Sitting back in her chair, Kathy took calming breaths in an effort to gather her senses and switched her computer on; perhaps focusing on work would help take her mind off her troubles, it usually did. Within five minutes, Kathy was engrossed in organising deliveries, checking over menus, ensuring that the tastes of their often demanding 'guests' were catered for, then remembered Dr. Mansard's efforts to grab her attention and made her way to his office.

Ten minutes later, tears welled at Kathy's lashes as she sat opposite Alexander, his hand curved gently over hers. Unable to confide in him about her completely inappropriate entry into Marcy Devereux's suite in the middle of the night, she had instead related the story of the vision in her room, of the woman standing in the corner. She omitted the names which still repeated as though on a loop through her mind. He had mentioned several techniques she could use to help quelle the anxiety.

"I've only been working here for the last ..." he checked his watch, "thirteen days, Kathy, but even I can see just how much effort it takes to run this place. My professional opinion is that you're exhausted! You need a break. When was the last time you took a holiday, and I don't mean one where you continued to work from home.?" She offered him a wry smile; somehow, he understood her exactly. Living at the house meant that she was on call twenty-four hours a day, seven days a week, and even when her deputy stood in on those days that were supposed to be her days off, she often remained at the house and popped into the office or opened up her laptop to finish something off, or answer another email. The guests' demands too, often broke into those times.

"I guess you're right." She brushed at an invisible piece of lint on her leg. Alexander's thumb caressed the edge of her palm. She allowed him to continue, enjoying the sensation of being touched – *it had been so long!* – and leant back in her chair. Their eyes met; his seemed so sensitive and understanding.

"Kathy, do yourself a favour ... take a few days off. Go anywhere. Book a city break, or a long weekend in a cottage. Somewhere with a log burner beside the sea, perhaps?"

She was instantly catapulted to a warm beach, walking barefoot through the sand, the water lapping at her feet, a child's hand, tiny and precious, in her own. The memory burned, and she pulled her hand back instantly as though scalded.

"Kathy?"

"I'm fine ... You're absolutely right. I do need a break, perhaps a weekend in Whitby, or up to Northumberland. I used to love going up there as a child."

Alexander's concern at Kathy's recoil melted away as she continued, assuring him that she would make arrangements for a few days off once Marcy had completed her treatment.

"Which is when?" he asked with a smile.

"Monday ... She leaves on Monday." The thought of the difficult television star finally packing her bags and leaving Hemlock House brightened Kathy's spirit, the relief surprising; she hadn't realised quite what an impact the woman's energy had had on her own. She rose with a genuine smile. Only three more nights, and Kathy would be waving goodbye to Marcy from the grand stone steps. Thanking Alexander for listening, she remembered that it was he that had wanted to see her. "Oh, Alexander, I'm sorry, but what was it that you wanted earlier?"

He threw her a gentle smile. "Nothing to worry about, Kathy. In fact, you've answered my question. I just wanted to know when Miss Devereux was leaving so that I could fit another therapy session in with her—to make sure she's in the right frame of mind before she starts filming."

CHAPTER NINE

With a soft tap at Kathy's office door, Eve, the owner of Hemlock House stepped in. Dark hair, greying at the temples, fell in wiry ringlets around a face that carried more than forty decades of stress and laughter lines. The afternoon light caught on skin pale beneath a summer tan.

"Was it a difficult passing, Eve?" Kathy asked with concern. Good friends for the last ten years, Kathy was used to the fall-out from Eve's deathbed vigils with the patients of Dove's Rest Hospice. Much of the time, Eve returned in a state of deep peace, but there were times, far more than she would like, when the passing of one of the hospice's terminally ill patients, or the private patients who sought her deathbed care, took its toll on the woman's gentle soul. Eve seemed distracted, jumping at the tapping of the apple tree on the window. "It's just the branch, Eve. Sit down, and let me get you a cup of tea," Kathy offered. She made quick strides to the tray and small kettle that sat on top of an ornately inlaid bureau, ready for when their small kitchen staff were too busy to attend to her needs, or on one of the many occasions when she and Eve worked late.

"No, Kathy. I'm far too wound up to sit."

Surprised at the tone in Eve's voice, Kathy stopped mid-stride. "Then what is it?"

"The names ..." Eve glanced around the room as though searching for something.

Kathy's arm tingled as though something crawled along it. She rubbed at her forearms. "The names I saw written on the wall?"

"Yes ... Oh, Kathy!"

Fear rose in Kathy's gut. "Eve, you're scaring me. Whatever is it?"

"They're the names of Barry Putchinski's victims."

"Victims? I've never heard of Barry Putchinski. Who is he?"

Eve swayed, a film of sweat glistened at her forehead.

"You're ill. For heaven's sake ... sit down." The colour had drained from Eve's face and Kathy guided her to the sofa.

After a few moments, Eve continued. "Barry Putchinski was one of my patients at Portland ..."

"The prison?"

"Yes. He died on my shift. I was with him ..."

The branch tapped again at the window making Eve start. Kathy covered Eve's hand with her own. Swallowing her rising fear, she made an effort to seem unaffected by the creeping dread falling over her. "I should have reminded Marlon to cut that branch. It makes me jump too!"

"Well ... I really should have told you this before, but Barry was also the previous owner of Hemlock House."

Kathy's hand tightened to a grip around Eve's and they both sat, hands clutched together, lost in their own thoughts for the next moments. The scene in Marcy's bedroom rose to burn in Kathy's mind. Nausea swirled in her belly. "Why was Barry ... incarcerated?"

Eve took a large breath, then spoke with her eyes closed. "He was a serial killer, Kathy. They called him the Fenland Ripper."

"But I've never heard of him! I've heard of Jack the Ripper, and Fred West." Her mind searched for the names of other

British serial killers and failed. "Ted Bundy, Jeffrey Dahmer, but never Barry Putchinski ..." Kathy mused, then asked, "The women that he killed ..."

"Yes, they were the women whose names you repeated to me."

"Did he kill them ...in this house?"

"Some, not all."

"I don't understand ... why would I see their names written across the wall in the Grace Kelly suite? Oh ..." Kathy's gut twisted. "Did he kill them in that room?"

"No. Perhaps ... I'm really not sure. I didn't delve too much into the grim details of his crimes - I particularly didn't want to know what happened in this house - but there was an unpublished biography ..." She shivered beneath Kathy's touch and her fingers gripped a little tighter, making the hold uncomfortable. "He did unspeakable things to those women, Kathy. Unspeakable!" Tension sat between them and Eve rose, then twisted on her heels to stare back down at Kathy; the fear in her eyes obvious. "I think ..." she said with a hand rising to her throat, "that Barry Putchinski has finally come back to haunt me!"

The remainder of the afternoon was spent reliving Kathy's experience, and Eve explaining hers: how she had been with Barry when he died, how he had begged to be free of the shackles that anchored him to his deathbed. "I told him though, that I couldn't take them off. It was against the rules, even in death ... it seems so cruel now, but he was a prisoner, a dangerous prisoner ..."

"You did the right thing, Eve," Kathy placated. "There was nothing else you could do."

"I did try to be kind, but touching him ... he was so repulsive, evil just wafted from the man, the energy in the room – I realise this now – was dark, black almost." She stopped for a moment lost in thought, or perhaps gathering the strength to continue. "Kathy, when he was dying, he recited the names ..."

"The ones I saw?"

"Yes, in exactly that order too. I've never forgotten a moment of those hours—they were so hideously terrifying. I was much younger then and didn't have the experience of death that I have now. If I'd realised that he was so close to death, knowing what I do now, then I would have made sure I wasn't alone."

"You did your best, Eve."

"I did, but Kathy, the way he screamed my name, the waves of pure hate ... and evil I felt as his spirit rose from his body ..." She stopped again. "I was so surprised, in such shock, when he left me the house."

"What?"

"Yes! He left Hemlock House to me ... and that's why I think he's back?"

"I don't understand."

"Don't you see? I didn't help him in his last moments!" Her anxiety rose to a peak. "All these years I've felt such a sense of ... guilt. I didn't take the shackles off when he asked me. I let him down. Left him to die tied to the bed, and now, now he's come back to take his revenge."

Tears flowed down her cheeks. Kathy embraced her friend, ringing her with gentle arms to damp down the emotional pain flowing through her. "There, there," she said patting her back as she would a crying child. "You did your best, Eve. What else could you have done?"

The apple tree knocked again at the window. Eve jerked, her head snapping to the noise. She scanned the room, eyes searching the walls and ceiling.

"Blast that apple tree! I'll ask Marlon to lop it in the morning."

As Kathy manoeuvred the sobbing Eve back to the sofa, a new name spoke in her memory; Meredith Blaylock. *Of course!* "Eve," she said with a renewed spirit. "I know someone who may be able to help!"

CHAPTER TEN

Providence House

As Kathy made the call to Meredith Blaylock and asked her advice about the horror that was unfolding at Hemlock House, Frankie lay curled in her bed, the duvet pulled up to her chin. A dull throb radiated from the base of her skull and up through to her temples. Puffy eyes stared back at her from the mirror on her wardrobe door and she turned away, loathing the woman reflected. She wiped at her nose as more tears flowed. Last night had been one of the worst of her life; seeing the loathing in Neil's eyes reflected in Sally's had been like a physical punch to the gut. When the event had been relayed to the rest of the crew their initial looks of shock had shifted to sideways glances, and then to avoiding her eyes altogether. Frankie had left the abbey with mortification smothering her like a shroud, Neil's accusations still ringing in her ears, and his disgust burning into her heart.

Cold fingers touched her cheek.

Frankie's breath caught in her throat as fear shot along already taut nerves. She darted a glance to her side, but no one stood there. Pulling the duvet closer to her chin, she checked around the room. The fingers had felt so real! She shivered, but not with cold. Unease settled over her self-pity and, with rising confusion, she left her bed, throwing on a hooded fleece, and padded through to the kitchen.

Behind her the door swung, wafting her ankles with cold air.

The sensation of being watched bore into the back of her skull and, as the hairs on her neck rose, she turned to the door. It showed no sign of movement. Just like the cold fingers on her cheek, its movement must have been a figment of her imagination. Panic curdled in her belly, rising to her chest. Her ribcage tightened, and her breathing became shallow. *Crazy! You're a crazy schizo! A crazy woman who sees things that aren't there.* She sobbed. Movement caught her attention as a shadow shifted along the wall. She froze. This time it was not in her peripheral vision, not something behind her that moved. This time it was a small shape, a figure perhaps, transparent, not quite there. She screwed her eyes tight shut, her heart tripping hard against her sternum, willing herself to open her eyes, and for the shadow to have gone. *It's just your imagination ... three ... you're having a psychotic break ... two ... it's not really there ...*

Tap! Tap! Tap!

The knocking made her heart leap, and when she opened her eyes, the figure had gone. The tapping increased to a series of irritated raps.

"Frankie!"

Sally! Casting a glance around the room, the shadow unseen, Frankie lurched to the door in two massive steps and threw it open. "Sally I ..." The words of apology, of self-flagellation, stuck in her throat; apologising would admit she had committed a crime. She buckled. "I'm so, so sorry! I didn't mean to hurt anyone ... the woman ... she-"

With a frown, Sally ushered Frankie back into her apartment, forcing her to sit on the sofa with gentle pressure. "Frankie, I won't beat around the bush ... I think that you're succumbing to the pressure of celebrity life-"

"I'm hardly a celebrity!"

"You're on the television, you have a public persona—that makes you a celebrity. We live in a rarefied world, Frankie. Many of my clients suffer with their ... nerves. They are creative, sensitive people who perhaps suffer more than most with their ... Now, don't get upset ... with their mental health." She paused whilst maintaining eye contact. "Now, I'm unsure quite what went on last night, but I know you well enough to understand that it wasn't ... deliberate, at least not in a malicious sense."

The tension that held Frankie in its grip eased a fraction. "It wasn't intentional at all, Sally!" Tears began to well as the memory of Neil's angry, pain-filled face stung again. "I saw the woman ... I had no idea about Neil's wife."

"It was an hallucination then?"

Frankie broke away from Sally's questioning eyes.

"Frankie, I've been in this business for more than twenty years. I've seen celebrities come and celebrities go, and the one thing that all those who have made a success in their career have in common – even after a meltdown – is that they talk about their problems and put coping strategies in place."

"Do you think I'm having a meltdown?"

"I know that you have a history of having ... of seeing things."

"Brooke!"

"Edward Brooke is not the most circumspect of individuals, Frankie. Quite the opposite, he's a notorious gossip!"

The knot in Frankie's already queasy belly tightened. "So, everyone knows?"

"No! But he made it his business to make sure that I knew about it. But I knew anyway, honey. You told me yourself, remember?"

Frankie eased a little more, although she wasn't ready to share her deepest concerns with Sally, at least not yet. "Do you … do you think I saw that woman because I'm so stressed?"

"It's possible. I've thought it through, and to me, the most likely scenario is that you've read something about the poor woman's death, or heard about it on the news, and pushed it into your subconscious, and with everything going on - the pressure to perform etcetera – then it resurfaced at an appropriate, or rather, inappropriate, moment. It's just an awkward coincidence that the description of the woman you saw was so similar to that of Neil's wife, but then so many women wear red lipstick and have blonde hair."

Frankie sagged back into the sofa, headache pulsing. Closing her eyes only intensified the pain.

"Frankie, I want you to pack your bags. I've booked you into a therapeutic retreat."

"How is booking into a spa going to help? I hate being massaged!"

"It's not that kind of a retreat; they specialise in celebrities struggling with their nerves … and they're very discreet, you'd be surprised at just who has stayed with them."

Frankie raised a brow, curiosity momentarily pulling her out of her self-pitying fug. "But I've got to work!" The pained glance Sally threw her was crushing. "They don't want me back, do they."

"Now, don't lose hope! Dean hasn't said that at all. However, we both agree that you need some time off—to rebuild your energies."

"Rebuild my energies! That's just a polite way of saying that I can't cope with the job."

"I'm sure you can cope, Frankie, but I think that perhaps you need a little help. Now ... I've spoken to Kathy at Hemlock House, and they're more than happy to have you stop with them for a few days. They have an excellent psychologist-"

"Psychologist!"

"Yes, someone you can talk to. Someone who can teach the tools you'll need to get yourself back on track."

Head thrown back on the sofa, eyes staring at the ornate plasterwork rose on her ceiling, Frankie ignored the shifting shadow in the corner of her eye as Sally continued to explain about the retreat whilst making them both a cup of sweet tea 'to help with the nerves'. The effort of ignoring the moving shape finally became too much, and she busied herself with packing her bags, grateful for Sally's company, her gossipy conversation a barrier between Frankie and the nagging worry that her mind was finally coming unravelled.

The final pair of trousers packed, along with her fleecy, very unglamorous, pink dressing gown and slippers, Frankie left her apartment. The opaque figure of a small boy, not more than eight years old, waved as she closed the door. She bit her bottom lip, swallowed down the yelp of terror and, with quick steps, followed Sally down the stairs.

CHAPTER ELEVEN

As Frankie left her apartment, Meredith slipped her car into third as she pulled out from behind the truck rumbling along the country road that would take them to Hemlock House. The busy streets of the town had given way to an open and rolling countryside of autumn leaves and black fields, and then to the broad and flat expanse of the fenlands in shades of brown and beige made dingy beneath the opaque sky. Reed beds with their waving fronds of nodding feathered heads hugged stalwart bulrushes, their chocolate brown heads exploding to a fuzz of creamy seeds

As Meredith pulled beside the truck to overtake, a car hurtled around the bend, and headlights aligned. Applying brakes with gentle pressure, Meredith returned to the space behind the truck. "Damn! Sorry Peter. I think my enthusiasm for this job is making me reckless."

Peter looked up from the notes in his lap, oblivious to the near miss. "Something happen?"

"Oh, I just nearly killed us, nothing to worry about."

Peter glanced at the truck blocking his view, then returned to his notes. "It says here that Hemlock House was the home of Barry Putchinski AKA the Fenland Ripper. He died at an institute for the criminally insane."

"Do they still call them that?"

"Probably not, but HMP Portland was originally built as just that, a prison for the criminally insane. It says it above the door. I've got an image of it here." He tapped the keyboard, pulling up the image of the prison.

"I'll look later, Peter. Got to focus on not killing us at the moment." Meredith pulled the car out from behind the truck once more. Ahead was an empty stretch of road without bends. She manoeuvred the car beside the truck, dropped a gear, then accelerated. "I remember the news articles when they caught him," she said as memories surfaced. "He was likened to the Yorkshire Ripper although, unlike Peter Sutcliffe, Barry was a man of wealth and status, well respected within his community." The car powered forward overtaking the truck with ease, and Meredith pulled back onto the right side of the road. "There. Did it, and we're both still alive."

Peter shook his head with a laugh. "I have every confidence in you, Meredith. You're a superb driver."

"Why thank you, Peter!" The next minutes passed without conversation as the car wove along the country roads, passing great beds of nodding reeds that stretched for miles. The flat surface of the land stretched to the gently rising slopes of the Wolds. Clouds cast dark shadows across the hills, and the sun, already weak, disappeared. In the far distance, storm clouds gathered, and the woodlands that stretched across the hills faded from dark green to black. Meredith shivered and turned up the heater.

"It's a long way out. The last village is miles back there."

"It is very isolated, which is why Barry was able to get away with murder for so long. His crimes spanned at least twenty years."

"He killed them at the house," Peter added scrolling through his notes.

"Yes. I'm a little hazy on the details, but - and you'll be able to correct me if I'm wrong - he killed one, possibly two, at another location."

"That's correct. The last two victims were taken to another property he owned, but only one died there."

"Remind me of how he was eventually caught."

"One of the girls he imprisoned at the other property managed to escape and alert the police."

"Ah, yes. I remember now! Odd that he should change his modus operandi in that way. As far as I know, and my knowledge of serial killers is limited, they're often creatures of habit."

"I think you're right. It is odd that he killed all the other women, at least seven that are known about, at his own home, and then started taking them to the other house. I wonder what changed? Let me just look ..." Peter tapped the keyboard of his laptop. "Damn! I've lost the connection. It's so far away from civilisation out here that I can't get a signal."

"Now that's where pen and paper are superior!"

"It's so much easier on a laptop."

"Well, perhaps we can get a connection at the house."

"I hope so! I was hoping to use a new spirit box app I downloaded yesterday. It's supposed to be very effective."

"An app?" Meredith's disconnect with technology was a source of great amusement to the technologically savvy Peter. "How on earth does that work?"

"Well, I've downloaded it onto my phone. I've got the latest Huawei eight- "

"In layman's terms please," she laughed. Meredith's mobile was an ancient oblong of virtually screen-free plastic that only took calls and received text messages. "You know it all bamboozles me! I'm old school darling!"

Peter returned her laugh. "Sure, but you know I don't have the same level of sensitivity as yourself. They don't talk to me the way they talk to you."

"And you know that they don't talk to me, Peter, not in words at least. It's more of an understanding that passes between us."

"Well, whatever it is, I don't have it-"

"Oh, Peter you do! You just haven't learnt to tap into it yet. I know you have a gift—you wouldn't be here otherwise." Meredith had understood Peter's sensitivity to the spirit world just as soon as she had met him. The aura that surrounded him sparkled, although sometimes with a dark energy, and the voice that so often spoke to her unseen, had whispered 'He has it. He knows. He's like you. He sees', ad nauseum until she had mentally blocked it off and focused on quizzing the man who had applied to join her first spirit investigation.

A colleague, who knew that Meredith was interested in witchcraft and the occult, although she had poo-pooed the idea that she had sensitivities as a medium, had pulled her aside in the teacher's lounge one break, and asked her, in whispered tones, if she believed in ghosts. The tremble in her colleague's voice was uncharacteristic, she being a blue-stockinged and stalwart spinster who took no nonsense from neither staff, parents, nor pupils.

Meredith had replied in low tones that she did. The sigh of relief from the woman was immediate. "Then, Miss Blaylock, do you also know how to get rid of them?"

"Well, I have been doing a little research lately. There are various ways that a spirit can be encouraged to leave, if they are becoming a nuisance."

"When would a ghost not be a nuisance, Meredith!" the woman had blurted, her terror obvious. Realising that she had spoken too loudly as Mr Gorman, the geography teacher, coughed on the smoke from his pipe, she took Meredith's elbow and led her to the far corner of the room and the paned window that looked down over the quad below.

"Well, some are benign."

"Not this one!"

"Oh?" Already intrigued, Meredith was now hooked. "You've had an experience then, Miss Bale?"

Blue eyes shining with fear, her skin without colour, Miss Bale had relayed the events that had begun to occur in her newly bought home, and become increasingly worrying over the past month, until in the past two days she had become convinced that a presence was haunting the house. "Things move, Meredith! And last night ... I woke to a man sitting on my bed!"

"Oh, Caroline! Did he hurt you?"

"No. He wasn't real—at least not in a physical sense! It was just the figure of an old man, a dark shadow. He just sat there for hours. I couldn't move. I just laid in my bed, with my covers pulled up to my chin until dawn, and then he just disappeared."

The woman's drawn face and red-rimmed eyes made sense now. "You must be exhausted."

"You've got to help me, Meredith. What shall I do? I've wracked my brains, but apart from calling Father O'Shaunesy at Saint Augustine's, I have no idea. I love my house, and the thought of having to sell it ..."

A moment of clarity had struck her then; Meredith did know what to do. She'd laid a comforting hand on Caroline's arm, offered her a room at her own home for the next few nights, then contacted a friend in the ghost-hunting community to ask for help. Enter Peter.

"You remember our first investigation, don't you?

"Of course, I'll never forget it."

"Well it was you who detected the spirit of Mister Thorpe."

"Oh, yes! So it was. But it was you who convinced him to leave and join his wife on the other side."

"True, but you are sensitive. You just need to stop hiding behind all your apps and gizmos and tune into the spirit's world instead."

Peter chuckled, as he always did when Meredith objected to his numerous ghost-hunting devices. "I'm a man, Meredith, we like gizmos."

"And that reminds me. You were going to tell me how this app works."

For the next five minutes Peter explained exactly how the app downloaded onto his mobile phone would help record and translate electronic voice phenomena, which many believed was the sound of spirits attempting to communicate with the living. Meredith had been sceptical, but some of the recordings Peter had achieved through his ghost box, as he called the hacked radio he used, were quite remarkable.

As the storm clouds gathered and rain began to spatter in earnest on the windscreen, the fenlands give way to the rising hills of the Wolds and an area of woodland. The car climbed between trees that overhung the road until a small sign, barely noticeable among the ferns at the roadside, directed them down a narrow track, even more heavily overhung with trees and banked by hawthorn and hornbeam. Peter continued to talk as the trees grew dense and the light faded. Meredith heard only occasional words as she focused on driving.

"And then we can use the laser trip wire-"

Peter's list of the devices brought for their night vigil, explanation of their application, and quite why he had chosen one make above another, came to an abrupt halt as the trees opened up to a clearing, and grey light once again flooded the car.

"Wow!"

The clearing gave way to a wide turning circle with an enormous statue at its centre on a central circular lawn. The house, entirely covered with ivy on the ground floor, rose to three storeys with attic windows in its steep roof. Wide stone steps led to a heavy panelled door beneath a porch supported by twin pillars. Below the ground floor windows were those that belonged to an obviously vast cellar. A double storey extension sat to the right, only just visible above a large hedge. The gardens to the side and back of the house were hidden behind the hedge, and the entire property was surrounded by mature woodland of huge oaks and sprawling horse chestnut.

Despite its grandeur, the house had an aura of decay that sat at the periphery of Meredith's awareness and presented itself as a whisper of unease she was only partially aware of. "I'm sure it looks beautiful when the sun is out."

"It's stunning. No wonder Barry Putchinski doesn't want to leave. It's the perfect abode for an evil serial killer."

"Oh, Peter! Do you really think it's that ... awful?"

"No, it's a beautiful house. I just meant that it's so isolated and huge, the potential for carrying out murder, and hiding the evidence, is massive."

Meredith reappraised the house; what had seemed like a beautiful place to spend a weekend suddenly took on a much more sinister nuance. The victims would have been brought here, presumably because Barry knew no one would hear their screams, or find their remains. She shuddered. "I see what you mean, but we can't assume the spirit is that of Barry Putchinski, Peter. As far as I'm aware, he's been dead a rather long time."

"Sometimes it takes a while for them to grow in power?"

"True, but I'd rather not make assumptions.

"Agreed."

Meredith followed the sign to the carpark, parking between a gleaming Range Rover and an immaculate Porsche. High-end cars filled the other spaces.

"Some serious money here!"

"It's an expensive place to stay."

"Plenty of bonkers celebrities by the look of it."

"Peter!" Meredith couldn't help laughing out loud, but then grew serious. "Kathy Fielding was quite adamant that we had to be discreet. I've had to sign a non-disclosure agreement."

"I signed it too, don't worry."

"She was also at pains to mention that she didn't want the guests to know about our visit."

"Right, but she's got ghosts howling through the night waking them up."

"As far as I'm aware, only Kathy has had an experience."

As Peter disappeared beneath the car boot to retrieve their cases, a petite woman with perfectly styled auburn hair, in an immaculate navy suit, opened the side door. Without waiting, she strode towards them with a tight smile.

"Meredith!"

"Kathy! It has been such a long time."

"It has, but so lovely to see you. Come on in."

CHAPTER TWELVE

The inside of the house was as impressive as the exterior and Kathy, the attractive redhead with immaculate style, ushered them through to the manager's office. The owner, Evangeline Maybank, prepared tea in the kitchen whilst Kathy perched on her office chair with a fixed smile as she glanced first at Meredith and then at Peter. He couldn't help notice that beneath the calm exterior, and despite the perfectly coiffured hair, she was wound as tight as a coil. Although Peter was unable to see an aura around the woman, unlike Meredith, it was obvious, even to him, that she was ill at ease and making enormous efforts to hide her discomfort.

She smiled again, mentioned that Mrs Maybank would only be a few minutes, and glanced at the door as though waiting for her saviour. Peter coughed, desperately searching his mind for something to say to put her at ease.

"Mrs Fielding, you have a beautiful house here."

"Miss," she smiled. "I'm not married ... although I was once ..." Flustered, a blush appeared on her cheeks, "but I find Mizz too ... aggressive I suppose."

"Sorry, I didn't mean to offend."

The woman's discomfort became even more intense. He made another effort to relieve the tension. "I've never been married, so just plain old Mister for me." He laughed at his own joke then became quiet as the two women merely frowned. "Men don't change their name ... it was meant to be funny."

Meredith patted his shoulder in a deliberately patronising way. "Don't mind Peter. I'm used to his little jokes."

As a smile began to curl on Kathy's lips, Peter sensed Meredith relaxing beside him. His own tension released then dissolved as the door swung open and Evangeline Maybank reappeared with a tray laden with a teapot, teacups, and a plate of biscuits. Several minutes later, a cup and saucer in one hand, a chocolate digestive in the other, Peter listened to Kathy's account of her experience whilst deciding whether it would be a faux pas to dunk his biscuit; he decided it wouldn't, and dunked the biscuit. His attention caught by Kathy's description of the apparition that had hovered above her in the middle of the night, the biscuit disappeared into the tea with an audible plop. He swallowed down the surge of fear that had passed through him as his imagination began to relive the moments so vividly described by Kathy, whilst hoping that no one had noticed the broken biscuit.

"And you say that it was a woman?"

Kathy's hand tightened around Evangeline's. "Yes, but she wasn't fully present. She almost looked like a projection—a still from a film just hovering in the corner of my bedroom - although her body wasn't as two dimensional as that would have- ... I'm sorry! I'm not making much sense."

"I understand exactly what you mean, Kathy."

"Thank you ... It was after the awful scene in the bedroom that I decided to make myself a cup of tea in the kitchen on that floor. It's such a large house that Evangeline very kindly installed a kitchenette for my use during the evenings. Whilst I was making the tea, I heard the thudding from the floor above and went to investigate. The noise, I was sure, was coming from the Grace Kelly suite where Marcy Devereux had been moved to because she had complained of feeling fearful in the first one."

Peter and Meredith exchanged a glance; Marcy Devereux would have to be put on their list of witnesses. He would leave quite how to broach the subject with Marcy, without raising her suspicions, to Meredith.

"I was concerned, given her state of mind, and the wailing and thudding coming from inside was just ... dreadful. So, I opened the door."

"That was very brave."

"Well, I didn't believe I had anything to fear."

"Even after your experience in the bedroom?"

Kathy swallowed; reliving the experience was obviously causing her discomfort. "Well, I was quite sure that it was just part of a waking dream. I'm not one given to fancy. I ... it was the book, a horror novel that had given me a nightmare. I didn't connect the two events, although I have to admit to feeling apprehensive."

"And what did you see when you entered the bedroom?"

"Oh, I was furious! Marcy had scribbled names all over the wall. I was certain that it was written with permanent marker."

"And was it?"

"No! It was all in my imagination. As soon as Marcy woke, the writing disappeared! I was horrified! At that point I believed that I was losing my mind."

"You didn't suspect that it was a spirit that had caused it?"

"No! I had no thoughts along those lines. It was only when Evangeline told me that the names were those of a serial killer's victims ..."

Meredith turned to Evangeline. "Ordinarily, we'd ask you to take readings over a number of weeks, but given the nature of Kathy's experiences, and the history of this house, Peter and I have agreed that the best way forward is to survey the house, and then put a plan of action into place. We begin this afternoon, if you're agreeable to that?"

"But ... you may be wasting your time! It may not happen again! Perhaps it is just my mind bowing under the stress of the past weeks?"

"I don't think so, Kathy," Evangeline replied kindly.

"It is entirely possible that you have imagined it, Kathy," Meredith added, "but I'd rather err on the side of caution and give the house a thorough check, and, if necessary, a cleanse."

Evangeline visibly relaxed. "So, it is possible to 'cleanse' the house if there is a ... spirit here."

"Indeed, it is," Peter added.

"Kathy, if we can return to you," Meredith continued. "Have you experienced any incidents before?"

"At Hemlock? No, and I've never seen anything before either although I've had one or two odd experiences in my life."

"Could you elaborate, please?"

"Oh, just a room I was shown years ago that I just couldn't enter. It had a horrible vibe. As soon as I stepped into the doorway, I felt it. And when I explained to the woman who was showing me around the house that I couldn't go in and had to leave, she said I wasn't the first to have had that reaction."

A broad smile curved on Meredith's lips. "That suggests to me that you are sensitive to the unseen world. It's all around us you know, but the majority are completely oblivious to it. From what you've told me, I believe that you are picking up on the energy of whatever entity has decided to pay Hemlock House a visit."

Kathy and Evangeline exchanged glances. Meredith waited, certain that they had something to share. When neither woman offered anything, Peter asked. "And you, Evangeline, do you have any experiences to share?"

"Well, I do have some. I have seen several ... spirits."

"Several ... so you're a psychic yourself then?"

"Oh, no! I don't think I'm sensitive in that way, but I have worked in a hospice and, besides running this place, I'm a Death Doula, so I have witnessed some odd ... happenings."

Peter raised his brows in surprise; it was the first time he had heard of the term used in England. He was aware that they existed in America, and that it was a growing business, but wasn't aware that it had crossed to England, at least not to rural Lincolnshire.

With a gentle laugh, and kind eyes, Eve said, "Yes, I'm your friend at the end."

"So not easily scared by spooks?" Peter's choice of words was deliberate; a litmus test for potential clients.

"I'm glad you've got a sense of humour, Mr Marshall. I had worried that you'd take it all horribly seriously and be all doom and gloom exorcists."

He returned her smile; many of their clients did want them to be 'doom and gloom exorcists'. "We take a gentler approach to the job, but take it seriously too. Our aim is two-fold; to return the house to a peaceful state, and also help the spirits pass on."

"And they do?"

"Generally speaking, yes."

"Not all hauntings are malevolent."

"True." Evangeline's hand travelled to her throat in what Peter took to be a nervous gesture. "But some are." Her eyes widened as a memory obviously troubled her, but the flicker of fear disappeared from her eyes as quickly as it had arrived.

Standing with her battered briefcase on the table, Meredith coughed. "If we may, Evangeline, a survey of the house is required before we speak to your guests."

Here again, the fear rose. "You will be discreet, won't you? I was so relieved to see that your vehicle is unmarked."

"Unmarked?"

"Yes, you don't have a logo, or advertising splashed across your car."

Peter laughed. "Like the Ghost Busters?"

Evangeline smiled for the first time, "I guess!"

"We promise absolute discretion, Mrs Maybank."

Kathy sighed. "Oh, good. We've lost two clients already this week, neither would say why they were leaving early but I suspect they became afraid."

"And the other guests?"

"So far, they haven't been affected. I do not know how, given the racket going on here last night—if it wasn't all just in my head!"

"Apart from Marcy Devereux?"

"I'm not sure. Our psychologist believes she's experiencing night terrors brought on by anxiety. She was on the verge of a breakdown, but seemed to be healing until the seventh day of her stay with us. After that, she started to display signs of extreme stress and then the night terrors began.

"Do you think she has seen the spirits then?"

"She had complained of feeling uneasy, and seeing something in her room. It was Doctor Mansard's idea to move her to a different suite so that the association with fear could be broken and the night terrors stopped."

"It sounds possible that she has had an experience ..."

"And also that her anxiety is causing the night terrors."

"And it's also possible that the other guests are completely unaware; some people simply don't pick up on it. What is audible to you, is not audible to them."

Kathy relaxed a little more. "Thank goodness. You see, the hotel isn't quite what it seems. We're very discreet, which is why many of our guests come here, but we treat celebrities, and those in the public eye when they're struggling with their mental health. It's a perfect spot here, secluded and quiet. They can recover without fear of intrusion, or their stories being splashed over the tabloids."

"Something like The Priory then?"

"Perhaps, although we don't treat addiction per se."

"You said that one of your 'guests' is in a terrible state?"

"I was referring to Marcy Devereux. I do hope you can do something to help. I have another two clients booking in later today and I can't afford to lose them. It takes a colossal amount of money to run this place."

A tap, tap at the window startled them all, and Peter's teacup chinked in its saucer, the tea flowing over the cup's sides.

"Damn that apple tree!" Kathy blurted. "Sorry! It gets me every time! I must talk to Marlon about lopping that branch."

Silence fell on the room.

"Well, if you're agreed, I'd like to start our survey of the house. I'd like to talk to your guests too, without making them aware of our purpose here, if that is acceptable, and tonight, after the guests have all retired to bed, Peter and I will hold a vigil.

CHAPTER THIRTEEN

The journey to Hemlock House - aka retreat for crazy celebrities - had been awkward. Sally had kept the conversation going, but her efforts at keeping the mood light had been obvious and stilted, and when she begun to delve into Frankie's experiences, and referred to them as hallucinations, Frankie sank into a state of emotional turmoil that was utterly draining. Convinced more than ever that her mind was finally breaking, she feigned sleep for the last forty minutes of the journey before sinking beneath consciousness ten minutes from their destination.

Having missed the narrowing, darkening approach to the house, Frankie opened her eyes to the huge edifice of a Georgian country mansion, its windows black and gleaming eyes, its door a gaping and cavernous mouth. She screwed her eyes tight shut against the monster, head throbbing.

"Wow! What a house. You are so lucky to get to stay here, Frankie."

Frankie opened her eyes; the house was just a house, the eyes just double fronted bay windows reflecting an overcast sky, the mouth just a pillared and canopied, front door.

A low throb at the back of her head accompanied the nausea of being startled to wakefulness as Sally had tapped her arm with a loud, 'We're here!' then swung her door open. Cold air gusted into the car's cosy interior, seeming to suck out its warmth in one breath and cover Frankie's legs with its icy touch.

"Come on, Frankie! I'm your agent, not your slave!"

At the back of the car, Sally placed Frankie's cases on the gravelled drive. The stones crunched underfoot as Frankie joined her then turned to view the house in full. It was immaculate. There wasn't a blade of grass poking from the gravel in the driveway. Each window frame was painted brilliant white, the individual panes of its Georgian sash windows were streak free, though their gleam was subdued by the overcast sky. Wide stone steps, aged and chipped, but clean of dirt, led to twin fluted columns beneath a flat-roofed porch. Beneath the canopy, a huge panelled door, black and glossy, carried a solid brass door knocker.

The swirl of nausea abated, but a queasy whirling remained in Frankie's gut as she picked up a case and followed Sally to the steps. A flash of yellow at a darkened pane and a woman's face, eyes accentuated by makeup, stared out from the window beside the door. Bright blonde hair, perfectly coiffured, sat as a halo around an expertly painted face. Their eyes locked and then the woman's mouth opened in a surprised 'O' before disappearing back into the room. It was a moment of mutual realisation as Frankie recognised the ageing star of various sit-coms, and now adverts, staring out at her from the retreat's window. Marcy Devereux! *So, she does have a problem!* Frankie remembered the gossip splashed all over the tabloids and low-brow magazines. In that moment of realisation came the understanding that perhaps her recent troubles too, would be broadcast among the public, on social media. YouTube, Facebook, blogs, newspapers, magazines, the list, and opportunity for humiliation, was endless. The tightness in her gut graduated to painful. Sally pulled back the door's brass knocker and tapped it against the doorplate.

"Sally, nobody knows I'm here, do they?"

"Only me and Carey, and you know how discreet he is. He won't say a dicky bird."

Slight relief. "Oh."

The heavy door swung open. A petite woman, smartly dressed in a navy-blue suit with a pinched-in waist answered with a bright smile. Lips painted a rich plum, with auburn hair curling beautifully around her shoulders, the woman had an air of pristine elegance that Frankie instantly envied; so collected, so sure of herself, so sane. The only tiny flaw was a slight puffiness about her eyes suggesting a sleepless night.

The hallway was wide, and the overhead chandelier cast a warm glow. At the centre a large table held a bowl filled with peonies. Picture perfect, its elegance was the opposite of the slightly stale, clinical entrance she had imagined on their journey. Taking a step across the threshold, Frankie experienced an emotion so intense that it made her gasp; Hemlock House, like its name, was poisonous.

CHAPTER FOURTEEN

The initial reaction to the house as Frankie placed a step across the threshold abated a little as the woman, who introduced herself as Kathy, took her through to the large lounge filled with velvet sofas and low coffee tables where Marcy Devereux had stared from the window. Flames danced in the open hearth, and the warmth of the room began to slough at the chill enveloping Frankie as she stepped through the front door. Heavy curtains embroidered with birds of paradise added to the feeling of luxury and comfort. A young woman, immaculate in black pencil skirt and snow-white blouse, asked if she would like a drink and passed her a menu. Scanning the list, coffee and ordinary tea were absent, and she chose a pot of camomile that claimed to 'help maintain a quiet equilibrium' instead. Her stay here would obviously be some sort of detox too. Sally asked for the same, quickly hiding her disappointment as she scanned the list with confusion.

"I can have a coffee on the way back home. I think I'll stop off at that lovely tea room we noticed in Caistor-le-Beck."

Frankie returned a polite smile, too exhausted now to rise to the challenge of small talk.

After their camomile tea, and Sally's continued assurances that everything would be alright once Frankie has rested, she kissed her on the cheek, followed it with a comforting hug, then left. Alone in the room, Frankie sank back into the sofa and waited. The chill crept back over her shoulders, and she moved to a high-backed chair closer to the fire. Mesmerised by the dancing flames and the tick of the large grandfather clock in the corner, she closed her eyes. The past days, weeks even, had been exhausting; the emotional turmoil, the mental scarring, the lack of sleep, had all taken their toll, and she drifted beneath consciousness, the cup and saucer still balanced in her hand.

Waking ten minutes later to the sensation of being watched, she opened her eyes with a start and was greeted by a wide smile of celebrity whitened teeth gleaming at her through layers of carefully applied make-up.

"It is you, isn't it?"

Like a zoo animal stared at through the glass of its cage, Frankie simply stared back.

"You're Frankie D'Angelo." The woman held out her hand. "I'm Marcy Devereux."

Sensing impending offence, Frankie returned the greeting with an enthusiasm she didn't feel and, as she took the proffered hand, said, "I knew it was you. As soon as I saw you through the window."

Marcy rewarded her with a huge smile, and laughed. "So sorry about that, but there's so little to do around here, any arrival is an excitement. It's all about being quiet and relaxed in this place." She gave the room a quick glance. "But I'm escaping the day after tomorrow."

"Oh?"

"Yes!" Her eyes glittered. "I'm starting work on my new soap – it's over in sunny Spain. I'd prefer it to be the French Riviera, but beggars can't be choosers."

Marcy Devereux, from the diamond rings on her fingers, to the beautifully cut clothes, and obviously designer shoes, looked anything but a beggar. Frankie struggled to think of something appropriate to say, her mind still fuggy from sleep.

"I'm sorry! I woke you, and you do look exhausted." Marcy began to rise.

Realising she didn't want to be alone in the room, Frankie asked her to stay, took a sip of her now cold camomile tea, and made an effort to rally herself and engage the woman in conversation. It quickly became obvious that the actress was a touch neurotic. Her energy was fractious and excited and, after half an hour of talking about her difficulties over the past months and the reason for her stay at Hemlock House, she confided in Frankie about how her life had been transformed by a new man who had 'dropped from the heavens' and 'turned a light on in her life'. She glowed as she talked of this newly blossoming romance, but remained tight-lipped about his identity. "I'll miss him, of course, but Spain really isn't that far away and we've planned it all out. I'll come back at weekends, and he has promised to come out to see me. Oh, Frankie ..." Her face was luminous with joy. "I really do think that this time – I've kissed so many frogs! – that this time, I've found someone special." She continued in raptures about how meeting him had given her new hope, and changed her perspective on life. Her enthusiasm was infectious, and she was surprisingly good company, with a quirky sense of humour, showing no signs of the difficult prima donna she was so well known for.

When a man slipped his head around the door and looked their way, Frankie gestured to Marcy with a silent 'is he the one?'. Marcy laughed and tapped her finger against her nose. Frankie returned the laugh, her mood lighter than it had been for several weeks.

Twenty minutes later, Marcy had finished a second cup of camomile tea and returned to her room, and the man who had peered around the door was now standing at the window and looking out across the gravelled driveway. Hedged by hawthorn and hornbeam that had been allowed to grow to full height, the view was limited, but gave the retreat the privacy and seclusion its fragile 'guests' needed.

With his back to her, Frankie watched him. Tall and broad-shouldered, jeans belted around a trim waist, he was obviously a man who took care of himself, very probably a celebrity. He turned, giving Frankie a good view of his profile; aquiline nose, full lips, nicely chiselled cheekbones, and a full beard carefully, but not prissily, trimmed. Hair auburn with a tinge of grey at the sides, he was an attractive man, and definitely a contender for Marcy's attentions though obviously a littler younger than the actress. Frankie couldn't place him among the celebrity faces in her memory. She took another sip of camomile tea as he turned to face the room—definitely very good looking in a casual, uncontrived way. Frankie decided that he was too natural to be a celebrity, and probably not Marcy's love interest either. She had alluded that he was well-off, and this guy, though dressed in smart casual, didn't have the look of being rich. The device that he held up to the window sealed it; he was a workman, someone brought in to do repairs perhaps? Sitting in the chair furthest away from Frankie, he offered her a friendly smile, then made notes in a pad, obviously recording the readings from the handheld device.

As she continued to watch him scribbling on his pad, he became aware of her gaze. Their eyes locked, and he held hers for a little longer than necessary, a flicker of puzzlement crossing his face. Frankie returned to staring into the fire, her cheeks beginning to burn. The man had stared at her like a rabbit caught in headlights, trying to remember where he had seen her before. Since her appearance in a well-known soap opera several years ago, it was a phenomenon she had experienced several times. The viewer would look at her in surprise, perhaps realising that they recognised her face, but unsure if she was a personal acquaintance, or perhaps a shop assistant, or someone they had met recently. They can't quite place her until a) they give up, or b) realise she's the actress who starred in that soap for a few weeks. Sometimes they would continue to stare as a broad smile crept up to their faces, other times they would look away, embarrassed to have been caught staring. Either way, it was an uncomfortable experience, one that she doubted she'd get used to, perhaps, given the current state of her head, one she wouldn't have to get used to. She sighed—every cloud! The man's cough startled her. In her moment of introspection, he had walked across the room and now stood only feet away. He gestured to the chair recently vacated by Marcy. "May I?"

Taken by surprise at his close proximity, and at how good looking he was now that she had a proper view, she replied, "Yes! Certainly. Please." Her cheeks began to tingle. *Calm down, Frankie!* Taking a quiet breath, she hoped he wouldn't notice her unease.

"Thanks." Device in one hand, notebook in the other he sat. The beautifully presented waitress arrived with her menu card. He made a joke about there being no coffee then ordered a green tea. "Apparently it will help to give me a glowing complexion!" He laughed, but Frankie noted the way he fingered the book in his hand; a classic sign that he was ill at ease too, even though perhaps only a fraction. The swallow that followed a furtive glance her way confirmed it. To break the tension, she reached a hand across the coffee table. "I'm Frankie D'Angelo."

He took her hand. "Peter."

"Hello Peter."

"Hello Frankie."

Both laughed.

Frankie broke the silence that followed, curious to know who Peter was and what he was doing at the retreat. "So, what are you in for?" The intrusive question was instantly regretted. "Sorry, that was crass of me!" Her cheeks burned.

"Oh, I'm not *here*! I mean ... I'm doing some work for the owner."

Frankie gestured to the handheld device. "With that?"

"Yes. I'm measuring the atmosphere, the temperature, that kind of thing. It's an old house. Georgian. And maintaining a positive atmosphere is ... important for maintaining its ... damp ... dry rot ... that kind of thing."

"Helping the conservation effort?"

"Exactly!" The word exploded with relief; he seemed as tense as Frankie felt.

"It is a beautiful house and lots of the features seem to be original. It must be a listed property, at least Grade II."

Peter nodded his agreement. "Yes, Grade II ... Have you noticed any areas that may need attention? I mean, areas where perhaps the atmosphere is a little ... dank, or cold?"

Without dwelling on the odd choice of words, Frankie recalled stepping over the threshold and the icy pall that had sunk over her. "Dank? No, but I've only been here for a few hours. I arrived this afternoon and haven't seen anything of the house apart from this room. It's cosy in here, in a grand and elegant way!"

"Ah! I see." The next moments were spent in silence as Frankie held Peter's gaze. She wanted to tell him about the experience of walking over the threshold, but that would out her as a crazy woman, and she couldn't bear the look of rejection that would follow. Peter had only been in her company for a few moments, but there was something about him that drew her to him. Green eyes, kind eyes, locked on hers, and her heart tripped a little harder.

She has to tell someone! "Peter, I-"

"Peter!" An older woman with a halo of curling silver hair, peered around the door. "Could I borrow you for a moment, please?"

CHAPTER FIFTEEN

Peter at her side, Meredith returned to the room allocated to them as a base for their investigations. Peter's case sat open on the elegant chaise longue beneath the room's tall sash window, its contents already dominating the room. There were black boxes of various sizes with numerous lights and dials, several 'hacked' radios and ghost boxes, cameras, some with night vision to enable them to record in total darkness, and others with full spectrum capacity, all designed for ghost hunting. These instruments, it was claimed, were able to see far beyond normal human sight. Meredith's own bag contained a spray of salty water, a temperature gauge, a paper bag with tied bunches of sage, a box of matches, and a Ouija board.

One of the gadgets that did meet her approval, was the meter used to detect changes in the electromagnetic field. On several of their investigations, where she too had picked up sensations, and that distinctive drop in temperature that signalled a spirit's presence, the meter had shown spikes. Peter had explained that the spikes were measured in milligauss, which was a unit of measurement of the magnetic field where spirit energy was believed to reside.

"Is the EMF meter fully charged?"

"It is." The meter sat on the pillow, ignored as Peter tapped at his mobile. "Wretched thing!"

"Problem?"

"Yes, well no, but I can't get this app to work."

"The new spirit box app?"

"Yes! My connection just keeps dropping. I'm afraid I won't be able to use it tonight. If I can't maintain a steady connection, then the readings will be hit and miss."

Meredith gestured to the numerous gadgets sprawled around the room. "We'll have to go old school then."

He tapped at the screen. "I'm sure this would work perfectly ..." He tapped again, then slid the phone into his back pocket. "You're right! We'll have to go old school. Fiddling around with the app is wasting our time." He checked his watch. "Six o'clock already!"

"It is, and we still haven't completed our survey of the house."

"It's so big, I don't think we'll be able to complete it today."

"True, but we need to at least do a quick sweep this evening before tonight's vigil." Peter gave an absent nod, his attention already focused on another piece of equipment and the tangle of wires attached to its back. "I hope you were circumspect when talking to the guests."

A mumbled 'of course'.

"Who was the young woman I saw you talking to in the lounge?"

"Frankie." His focus shifted to the view beyond the window, distracted by his thoughts. His aura fizzed. Meredith rolled her eyes. "What excuse did you use?"

"Oh, that I was here to help maintain the property; she thinks I'm some sort of conservationist, and I guess we are, we're just trying to stop the rot in a different kind of way."

Meredith laughed. "That's the first time I've heard a haunting being referred to as a rot, but I think you're exactly right. If the spirit - if it is malevolent - is allowed to gain a hold here, then the energy of the place will decline, along with its fabric. Do you remember Marsh House?" An inner shudder as she remembered the dilapidated house bought by an unsuspecting property developer. Abandoned for five years, the house had entered an unusually rapid decline, which was especially marked given that it was a new build. Meredith's investigations had uncovered the fact that a man had been murdered by his wife in the house and she had then taken her own life. The house had changed hands three times in those five years, each time being occupied for just a few months at a time, and the last owners had stayed for only one week. They were reluctant to speak to Meredith at first, but she had hidden the fact that she was working for the current owner to whom they had sold the property, and they had eventually relented and spoken to her at length about their experiences there. After listening to their story, Meredith was certain a malevolent spirit, that of the sadistic and murderous wife, was in residence at the property.

She had returned to the house, which seemed in an even more dilapidated condition than on her previous visit, and attempted to cleanse it. Her efforts had failed, and the building had been condemned three months later, and then demolished. The area where it had once stood was now a patch of scrubland with a large 'For Sale' sign. A new house on the building plot was inevitable, but Meredith doubted it would be free of trouble.

"Do I ever!" Peter gave an exaggerated shudder. "That was one creepy place."

"And completely destroyed by the malevolence of the energy that filled it."

"Do you think that will happen here?"

"Until we discover what kind of spirit has decided to pay a visit, then it's hard to say."

As Peter continued his efforts to untangle wires, Meredith's thoughts returned to the younger woman in the lounge. From the energy that had sparked around Peter's aura when Meredith had mentioned her name, the woman had had quite an impact on Peter. "So, the lady in the lounge ... did she have anything useful to say?"

Catching the lilt in her voice, Peter flashed Meredith a glance, unable to keep a smile from curling onto his lips. He quickly re-focused on the tangle of black plastic worms. "No. She hadn't noticed anything. She's only been here a few hours."

"And her name?"

"Frankie."

"Frankie? ..." Meredith prompts.

"... I can't remember! D-something."

Meredith tapped a finger against her chin. "Her face *is* familiar ... but I can't place her. Do you recall seeing her on TV?"

"No. And I didn't like to ask."

"You did the right thing. We're not here to pry on the guests; that is the very last thing Evangeline wants us to do."

With the black wires unravelled, Peter held the device up in triumph. "That's the last camera sorted. I can set up a full system. I've brought the infra-red and the full spectrum cameras with me. Once we decide where we want to film, I can set them up."

"Do you think that's wise?"

"How else-"

"What I mean is, that if we set up the cameras-"

"Which we need to do, to catch evidence of any phenomena."

"Absolutely, but if we set it up with all the wires and tripod etcetera, and a guest decides to go walkabout ..."

"Oh, yes, I see what you mean."

"We need to keep the equipment to a minimum, perhaps just one that can be easily moved if necessary. Evangeline was adamant that the guests shouldn't be alerted to our work."

Silence sat between them for a moment as Peter mulled over the problem. He broke the silence. "Then we should do it in full view!"

"Surely that defeats the object."

"Not if we have a good enough excuse. We could set up the equipment and explain that it is part of a maintenance programme and needs to be in place for twenty-four hours, apologise for any inconvenience, and then take our readings without fear of being caught taking sneaky photographs and readings, or spooking the guests." He made a small chuckle at his own joke.

"That's a great idea, Peter. I think you're absolutely right."

A broad smile broke across his face. "Excellent. Then I suggest we continue our survey of the house. He pulled a sheet of paper from the bed. "The business manager has drawn a map of the building. I've counted forty-five rooms, and that doesn't include the cellar or the attic, of which there are both. There are three staircases. We've seen the grand staircase that leads off from the hallway, but there is another staircase that leads to the main house, and another at the back that originally led to the servants' quarters. It's a labyrinth, Meredith."

Meredith scanned the maze of rooms drawn onto the map. It detailed three floors, along with the cellar, and the attic, and several sprawling extensions added over the three hundred years since the house was built.

"There's no way we can cover all of that space in the few hours we have left."

"We can't, so we'll have to be smart."

"Oh?"

"We should find out exactly where Barry Putchinski killed his victims and focus on those areas. I think that those rooms are the most likely candidates for picking up on supernatural activity."

Meredith recalled the fear that had flickered in Evangeline's eyes when she had spoken about the serial killer and her statement that she hadn't delved too deeply into quite where in the house the 'incidents' had taken place. "I can talk to Evangeline, although I expect some resistance there, but we also need to read the police reports if possible, and any articles that were written at the time. It may be useful to track down the original investigating officer too."

"Agreed. I'll start reading the material I've already downloaded."

CHAPTER SIXTEEN

After reading through the notes he had collected in a folder on his laptop, and then attempting a search on the internet for any more articles regarding the Fenland Ripper, Peter had been disappointed by the lack of information about precisely where the women were murdered in the house. Eventually, he decided to set up his ghost hunting equipment along the corridor where Kathy had her initial experience of the writing on the wall.

Marcy Devereux had been moved to a third suite of rooms, and the guests had been informed that Peter was taking essential readings as part of the conservation efforts of the Grade II listed Georgian country home, the lie necessary in order not to arouse their suspicions or concerns.

As part of the survey, temperature readings had been taken of the ground and first floors, but apart from a particularly cold room in a modern extension at the back of the house that Peter noted as of inferior construction, there was no indication of anything unusual in the rooms and corridors. However, given the large size of the property, and the limited time since their arrival, only the ground floor and second floor where the phenomena were reported as having happened, had been surveyed. The remainder - two large extensions, the first floor, attics, and cellars - were yet to be inspected.

Cameras were set up to capture movement along the corridor outside the room where Kathy saw the writing on the wall. Inside, was another set of interlinked equipment. One camera pointed to the wall, another to the bed, another with a wide-angle, full spectrum lens, was set at the far wall to capture as much of the room as possible. Motion sensors, thermal cameras, electro-magnetic meters, were all set up to capture any evidence of ghostly activity during the vigil. Despite his best efforts, Peter had been unable to get a reliable signal for his mobile and so his ghost box app was useless, forcing him to use the audio equipment to pick up any electronic voice phenomena and translate it through a less techy ghost box.

With the camera and video system finally set up, Peter drank coffee from his flask and waited for Meredith to return from her interview with the owner, Evangeline Maybank. The woman's role as a Death Doula fascinated Peter, and he was more than curious about her experiences. He could understand sitting with someone you love as the time to pass drew near, but not repeatedly, with strangers, through choice. Sure, if you were a carer in a hospice, it would be a regular event, but they were paid employees, whereas Evangeline did it voluntarily—gratis. Before the investigation was over, he decided, he would find a way of broaching the subject without appearing to pry.

Taking another sip of coffee, and brushed by a chill, he stuffed his free hand into his jacket, and continued to wait for Meredith. He checked his watch; twelve forty-five am. He took another sip of coffee, and listened to the house as its ancient timbers creaked. Footsteps alerted him to Meredith's return, and he moved out into the corridor to greet her, eager to know if Evangeline had given them any information about Putchinski's activities during his twenty-year career of murder at the house.

As he stepped out into the corridor, expecting to see Meredith emerge from the staircase, movement caught his attention. It was not Meredith. A quick glance confirmed his fear; his camera was facing in the wrong direction, and opposite to where the figure stood. Resisting the urge to reach out and twist the camera around on its tripod, he forced himself to wait, remaining absolutely still. The figure shifted in the shadows as Peter slipped a hand into his pocket to pull out his mobile. He thumbed the screen whilst watching the figure, squinting in an effort to focus more clearly; why did ghosts always appear in the dark! The figure seemed to hover and sway. Peter held his camera up and clicked. The flash filled the space with intense white light and when his eyes adjusted the figure had gone. Without waiting to look at the image captured on his phone, he ran to his full-spectrum camera, took a photograph, then ran down the corridor, pulling out his meter, and pointing it at the space where the spectre had been. The dial jumped. A silent 'Yes!' and he continued down the corridor. As he reached the third bedroom along the hallway, the reading dropped. He scanned the space ahead but, seeing nothing, turned to walk back to the room with his equipment. The dial jumped once more and, from the distance, came the muffled sound of footsteps on the stairs. Heartbeat tripping, he walked back to the bedroom with the meter; the dial still pointing to the higher end of the scale. At the doorway, the light for the EMF reader flashed green. Another silent 'Yes!' and he swung to the increasingly loud footsteps on the stairs. This time he would be ready! Standing behind the full spectrum camera, he snapped an image as the figure finally reached the top of the stairs. Flashlight filled the space once more, but this time it was accompanied by a quickly stifled yelp.

"Peter!" Meredith hissed. "You've blinded me."

As his vision cleared, and the hallway returned to grey, he discerned the figure of Meredith, hand clasping the bannister, with one foot on the top riser, paralysed by the blinding flash. A small torch shone a bright circle on the opposite wall.

"Sorry!" The ghostly spectre momentarily forgotten, he offered his hand and guided Meredith along the dark landing.

"It's not like you to be so jumpy, Peter. Has something happened?"

"It has! I've seen my first ghost."

"You have?"

"Yes, it was standing a little further down the hallway from the top of the stairs. A dark figure that I'm certain was a man. I could only see an outline, his face was in complete darkness, but I think he was wearing a cloak. And ..." he paused for effect, "I've got a photograph!"

"Yes, of me!"

"No ... well, yes, and sorry! I thought you were him, the EMF meter picked up a spike in milligauss along the corridor, and then I heard footsteps again. Sorry, I'm rambling. Anyway ..." He pulled out his mobile phone and scrolled to the last image taken. "I've got a photograph of the spectre." As Peter held the mobile for them both to see, Meredith pulled glasses from inside her jacket, and peered at the screen. The image showed the top of the staircase and part of the corridor. The bannister's glossy varnish reflected the light, the walls were bleached out, the carpet seemed to shine, and at the very right edge of the image was a fold of dark fabric, illuminated from the shadows by the flash. "There! There it is. I knew it was a cloak." Peter zoomed in on the image, focusing on the black fabric. "And look there. Is that a boot?" Meredith peered closer. "I'm not sure, Peter. It could just be a trick of the light creating that effect."

"But that's exactly where I saw the man standing. He disappeared as soon as the flash went off."

"Perhaps."

Surprised at her scepticism, Peter continued, "I'll upload it to the laptop. We can get a far better look at it on there. Plus, there is the feed from the EVP recorder."

"The more evidence we have the better."

"You're very downbeat about this, Meredith!"

"I'm very excited, Peter. That's the truth, but I don't want my excitement to hamper the investigation. We need to keep a level head about us."

"You're right," he replied. "But my first sighting, Meredith! And it was so clear."

"Upload the image to the computer, and I'll take a proper look."

The next ten minutes were spent uploading the image and EMF readings. The image enlarged on the laptop's screen was no clearer; the black area on the image could be the edge of a cloak and possibly a boot too, but Peter's hand was unsteady when he took the photograph, and the image too fuzzy to be sure. Disappointed, Peter turned to the EMF meter. "It definitely shows a spike." He took Meredith through his paces: how he walked after the spectre until the readings dropped, and then returned along the corridor, the readings elevating once more. "And that's why I thought you were a ghost. The footsteps along with the elevated reading, and the experience I had just had-"

"Completely understandable. It's interesting that the readings were increasing as you approached this room though. How are they reading now?"

Peter removed the lead connecting the gauge to his laptop and switched the device back on. "It's registering disturbances in the electromagnetic field."

"So, that indicates that there is a presence ... here." Meredith scanned the bedroom recently vacated by Marcy Devereux. The aroma of her intense perfume still lingered.

"I think that's exactly what the meter is registering."

Peter moved around the room ensuring that all of the equipment was functioning.

The ghost box crackled.

They exchanged a quick glance then stared down at the box perched on Peter's laptop case.

Static crackled again and was followed by a wheedling whine.

Peter and Meredith continued to stare at the box. Peter's heart tripped. The light from the box was not lit, the power cable remained unplugged. Meredith's fingers grasped his sleeve.

"Is that noise coming from the box?"

"It is."

"But it's not plugged in."

"I know."

Both stood frozen. A chill brushed between them, and Meredith's hair blew in an unseen breeze. The gauge in Peter's hand registered at the highest end of the scale.

"There's something here!"

A low wail rose from the box. Muffled and threaded through with static, a voice twisted like a tendril of smoke into the air. The hairs on Peter's arm prickled. The noise continued, the words indecipherable, the lament obvious.

"I can't understand it."

"Is it singing?"

As Peter pressed 'record' on his mobile, the ghost box became silent. "Great! It stops talking just as I start recording the evidence!"

CHAPTER SEVENTEEN

By ten o'clock, Marcy had finished her cup of hot chocolate, enjoying its thick sweetness and the warmth of the drawing room's fire. She had even enjoyed the company of Patsy Turlington, at least until the woman began to talk about her husband, and then her therapy sessions. Theirs had been a wonderful marriage, Patsy had confided, despite his roving eye, although in the last year before his death they experienced a 'rocky patch'. His heart attack on stage at the Plowright Theatre during one of the tricks he had begun to take far too much pleasure in - sawing her in half - had been a terrible shock. It wasn't until Patsy began to talk of Dr. Mansard and how he had helped her put everything into perspective, made her feel as though she could conquer the world, or at least make a success of a career beyond the shadow of her husband's, that Marcy's interest wavered. When Patsy began eulogizing about how 'amazing' and 'wonderful' the man was in breathy tones, and 'so understanding!', and 'those eyes!', Marcy had felt a flicker of jealousy, made her excuses, then retired to her rooms. Dr. Mansard *was* 'amazing' and their therapy sessions always made her feel so much better, so much stronger and able to face the world again. She had berated herself for being so silly; the man was only doing his job, and she should be happy that Patsy was benefitting from his expertise too. It was just that he had made her feel *so* special, unique in fact. That he had made Patsy feel the same way, grated.

Despite ruminating on her conversation with Patsy, and worrying that sleep would bring more nightmares along with the names that kept repeating in her head, she fell beneath consciousness within five minutes. Her dreams, when they came, were dark and full of foreboding.

She woke with a jolt hours later, immediately aware that someone was in her room. A cold finger brushed her cheek, and then a voice whispered in her ear.

CHAPTER EIGHTEEN

The fitful sleep that Frankie fell into was broken once more. After a bedtime drink of hot chocolate gladly accepted from the gentle owner of the retreat, she took a hot bath, washed and dried her hair, gave herself a facial using the complimentary face masks found on the well-stocked bathroom shelves, and then wrapped herself in her pink, decidedly unglamorous, fleecy dressing gown. She pulled on her fluffy socks and sat beside the fire as it burned in the bedroom's hearth. Unable to switch off, she took out her mobile, and tried once more to connect to her roaming data. The mobile failed, and she slipped it back into her pocket with a disgruntled sigh. There was absolutely nothing to do at the retreat: no television, no Wi-Fi, no phone. Completely cut off from the outside world, she couldn't even play a game of solitaire on her mobile.

Kathy, the retreat's immaculate manager, had explained that all stimulants, including tea, coffee, and alcohol were prohibited at the retreat, and that ban extended to the television, mobile phones, laptops, and the internet in general. This, she had been told, was to help reduce the over-stimulation, and broken sleep, that many of the retreat's residents suffered from. Their time at Hemlock House was to be a complete 'down time' where they focused on understanding their deepest needs, began constructing the foundations of emotional resilience, and developed a good sleeping pattern, along with healthy eating habits. Outside stimulation, Kathy had insisted, was a complete block to that. Frankie could, Kathy had offered, take long walks in the gardens; the grounds were extensive and full of fascinating 'rooms' designed specifically to ease tension and help her take joy from the natural world, itself a powerful source of healing. The woods were mature and perfect for rambling through, and there was a stream where she was welcome to fish. There was also a gym at her disposal, and shelves full of books that she was welcome to read. Music therapy was also prescribed, and they had a room for that too.

Frankie pulled the robe a little tighter as a chill crept along her neck, and scanned the books in the case beside the fire. Stocked with novels, she picked Daphne Du Maurier's *Rebecca*. The image of the house on the cover looked surprisingly similar to Hemlock House – vast, sprawling, and ominous, and locked behind iron gates.

The initial unease on entering Hemlock House had turned to panic once she realised that Sally's departure left her without transport. She was trapped at the house, her own car locked in the carpark at home. For the first time since passing her driving test at the age of seventeen, she was unable to go where she pleased, when she pleased. She read the first page of her book standing in front of the fire as her eyelids grew heavy, then climbed into bed, propping herself with pillows, duvet drawn up to her chest. The words seemed to melt on the page and her eyelids lowered.

Thirty minutes later, she woke with a start to a thud that was quickly followed by a creak as though pressure was being applied to the joists in the ceiling above. She waited for the thudding to repeat, but the timbers only creaked and, after several minutes, she drifted back into a light sleep, the parted book resting on her chest. An hour passed and she woke with a jolt. As she sat, the book slipped from her hands and fell to the floor. The light remained on, the fire burned down in the hearth, and from somewhere in the house she heard someone crying - a woman - the tone of the voice too high to be that of a man. The sob increased to a wail as she pulled the light cord, plunging the room into darkness, and lay back down to sleep.

The fire's dying embers glowed orange, their light pushing back the dark shadows around the hearth, and Frankie listened to the sobs, wondering if it was Marcy Devereux, or one of the other celebrities she had caught a glimpse of today. Along with at least one man, there were another two women staying at the house although, given the size of the place, there could be dozens. She recognised one of the women as an elusive former child star caught drink driving several years ago. The news had been splashed all over the tabloids and cheap gossip magazines. The other woman was Patsy Turlington, the widow, and former glamorous assistant, of a celebrity magician. Since his death, and the end of the television show, the merry widow had done everything in her power to gain work in the industry and had even managed several weeks on *I'm a Celebrity ... Get me Out of Here!* and *Strictly Come Dancing*. The signs of stress had been evident only last month when the woman had raged at the show's more acerbic judge as he had savaged Patsy's wooden efforts at the Samba. Backstage she was caught on camera tearing at her beaded dress, mascara already running, screaming expletives at a terrified production assistant.

Despite the lack of television and internet, Frankie's day tomorrow was fully booked: a walk around the grounds was to be followed by breakfast, a consultation with the shrink, and then a session with the beauty therapist. Lunch was to be followed by a therapy session, another walk or gym visit, and then a beauty treatment. The thought of endless activities, both mental and physical, was draining.

The thudding and the wail of self-pity repeated. Frustrated, and disturbed by the heart-rending noise, she grabbed her dressing gown, pulling the cord tight about her waist, and left her room, intent on discovering just where the noise was coming from, unsure if she should do anything about it even if she did discover its source.

As she left the room, the voice grew faint. She stopped to listen. The wailing continued, louder as she stepped back into her room suggesting that perhaps it was coming from the room above, or below, her own. She followed the dimly lit corridor to the stairs two bedrooms beyond hers. The wailing grew louder as she approached the landing. Footsteps could be heard treading on another staircase, or perhaps inside a room. As she reached the landing, a figure stooped, stood tall, then disappeared into a bedroom. Moments later it reappeared, torch in hand. The distinctive shape of a tripod loaded with a camera was clear as the man shone the torch at the equipment. Frankie took a step forward. The man swivelled, and blinding light was accompanied by the pop and whine of a flash.

"Who's there?"

"Hey!"

"Sorry!"

Shielding her eyes against another potential flash, her blinded sight returning, Frankie waited at the top of the stairs.

"I'm sorry! Have I woken you up?"

Peter, the conservationist from the drawing room! "I heard thudding, but unless you were doing a tap dance above my head then I don't think it was you who woke me up." She took steps towards him as he remained silent, his hand on the camera, with a look on his face that suggested it couldn't decide if it was a smile or a grimace, it was definitely confused. As he struggled to reply, she gestured to the equipment. "What is it that you're measuring? The manager said that you were setting up equipment and not to be concerned. Is it damp up here or something?"

Peter nodded as he replaced one of the meters inside his pocket. "It is."

"You must be keen ..."

"Keen?"

"Yes, to be working this late."

"Oh, well ... yes. We decided that working at night was the best way to get the job done with the minimum intrusion ... we didn't want to get in the way of the guests ..."

"Where's the other one?"

"Other one?"

"Yes, the woman who is working with you. Doesn't she have to work through the night too?"

"She was with me until half an hour ago, she's gone back for a rest."

Stepping over wires as he walked towards her, he ushered her along the corridor, arm outheld like a shepherd herding its flock. "I'm truly sorry that I woke you. I'll try to be quieter."

"It's okay. I don't think it was you. This house ... it's old ... so many thuds and creaks, and I thought I heard someone sobbing."

"Oh?"

"Yes, I'm pretty sure it's one of the other guests. I'm not sure if it was the thudding above me or the crying that woke me, but I came to see if I could help."

"And you heard it from here?" As he motioned to the space, torchlight illuminated the walls.

"Yes, to be honest, I thought it might be Marcy Devereux, probably because she's the only other guest I've met so far."

"Oh."

"Did you hear anything?"

"... No ..."

An awkward silence fell between them and Frankie berated herself for speaking so freely; the man was obviously not interested. "Well ... goodnight."

He mumbled a 'goodnight' and returned to his equipment, shining light on a black box, and Frankie, feeling the chill of night brush over her, and realising she had been talking to him in her definitely unglamorous dressing gown, stepped back down the stairs.

CHAPTER NINETEEN

As Marcy Devereux was lifted by unseen hands from her bed, the wailing began again, and Frankie froze with one hand on her bedroom door. It was definitely a woman crying, and she sounded to be in such pain, as though her heart would break. Unsure if it was the neurotic Marcy, or, perhaps more likely the unstable widow, Patsy Turlington, she entered her own bedroom, switching the light on with relief. The fire had died back to embers, but the room remained warm. The wailing continued, rising and falling as an undulating babble. Whoever it was, was really suffering, and surely attention seeking! She decided it must be the widow, and returned to bed. The minutes passed, and the wail continued, and Frankie turned the light back on. Her watch read three seventeen am. Head throbbing with fatigue, she pulled the duvet to cover her ears, and closed her eyes against the noise. It continued as a perpetual whine, tugging at her conscience.

Minutes passed until, with an exasperated 'For heaven's sake!', she threw back the covers, and left her room to trace the noise and offer help to whoever was making the awful racket. No doubt, they wouldn't appreciate her 'help', but there was no way she could sleep. When she turned up, perhaps they would realise just how noisy they were being and try to keep their emotional pain a little more under control! Tightening the dressing gown's belt, slippers on, she followed the noise along corridors and up several flights of stairs, turning the lights on as she passed each switch; the place was creepy enough without walking in the dark too.

As she took another flight of stairs in what must be another wing of the labyrinth-like house, a brush of cold made her shiver, and a draft caught the bare skin at the nape of her neck. She slowed, listening; the voice seemed to have been joined by another. Their words were indecipherable; an angry, whining, babble. The voices faded, replaced by a woman crying. The source of the noise seemed to come from further along the landing where light seeped from beneath a door. Unable to ignore the pain in the voice, she grasped the handle, and opened the door. The room was filled with stark light that bleached out everything apart from the wall ahead. Frankie's grip on the handle tightened. The wailing faded to silence as she stared at a wall scrawled with signatures—names written in crimson ink on mottled wallpaper, marked by rings of damp, and covered in an old-fashioned pattern of pink rosebuds and tendrils of ivy. The hands were shaky, but legible, and had written the names of eight women on the wall: 'Barbara, Noelle, Mary, Doretta, Annie, Betty, Doris, Marcy'.

The light dimmed, diminishing until the low wattage bedside lamp was the only source. A moan rose from the bed. The hairs on Frankie's neck crept as the light closed in and Marcy Devereux appeared centre stage. Spread-eagled as though tied to the bed's posts, red welts ringed Marcy's wrists and ankles. She writhed against invisible restraints.

"Ms. Devereux!" Frankie took a step towards the bed, keen to wake the woman from her night terrors, but unsure of the protocol in these situations; were you supposed to wake them, or were you supposed to leave them? She had a vague recollection that you weren't meant to wake sleep-walkers, but did that also apply to night terrors? The woman was obviously in some imagined agony.

"Marcy!"

The woman writhed, and a low wail filled the room.

"Doretta!" she hissed. "Annie! ... Ohhh, D-o-ris!"

The hairs bristled on Frankie's neck as Marcy continued to recite the names scrawled on the wall, although her lips didn't move, and the voice didn't seem to come from her mouth.

"Barbara ..."

"Marcy! Marcy, wake up!"

"Noelle ... Mary ... Doretta ... Annie ... Betty ... Doris ... Marcy ... Marcy ... Marcy ..."

As Marcy continued to struggle and moan, repeating the women's names, the spotlight faded and the room grew dark. Silver moonlight from a window bare of curtains shone across an unmade and empty bed. Frankie stared at the greyed-out and empty room in disbelief.

Icy fingers stroked Frankie's cheek and she jerked back from the doorway, pulling the door closed with a dull thud. Still reeling from the vision, she ran back to her own room, turning on all the lights and locking the door. Duvet pulled tight over her shoulders, the names of the women scrawled across the wall, repeated in her mind.

• • • •

UNAWARE OF FRANKIE'S terrifying vision, Peter continued to record the temperature and magnetic field of the rooms where his equipment had been set up. Apart from the earlier exciting readings that he was sure were a sign of a ghostly presence, and the hideous noises emanating from the disconnected ghost box which Meredith assured him were absolutely, one hundred percent, evidence of ghostly activity, the night had been uneventful, and the only temperature drop he had recorded was what he would expect within the house as the night grew cold. He thought back to his conversation with Frankie D'Angelo, wishing that he could have shared exactly what he was doing with her, if only to keep her talking a little longer; there was something about her that he found immensely attractive.

Before dawn broke and the staff began to arrive to take care of the retreat's guests for another day, Peter packed away his equipment into the two holdalls and one rucksack that he had crammed them into. He had attempted to negotiate leaving them all intact and running during the day, but the owner had insisted that they be out of sight of the guests. Meredith agreed, arguing that they could perhaps be tampered with in their absence. Eyes rimmed red, and with an enormous yawn, he zipped the final bag, hauled the heavy weight over his shoulder, and returned to the B&B for a few hours' sleep then an intensive afternoon of analysing the data collected during the night.

CHAPTER TWENTY

Exhausted by the day's upheaval, Kathy had slept well despite a heightened state of anxiety enveloping her like an itchy glove. She had woken at dawn to birdsong and the tapping of the apple tree at the window of her bedroom. Berating herself for not having spoken to Marlon, the groundskeeper, she showered, dressed, and was in her office by six-thirty. She checked through the guest list, noting any dietary requirements, and hurried to the kitchen to pin the list on the board ready for Karen to read before she started preparing breakfast, with a note that next week two more celebrity guests, one a vegan with an eating disorder, the other a pescatarian with nut allergies, would be arriving for a ten day programme of therapy. She continued her morning by checking the communal rooms to ensure all were spotless and that the cleaning rota, with its hourly, daily, weekly, and monthly tasks was being adhered to, then welcomed the guests as they trickled into the breakfast room during the morning. By ten o'clock her head was thumping. Evangeline had yet to make an appearance. The ghost hunters were absent, as was Marcy. She made enquiries after Marcy. It was unusual for the woman to miss breakfast, and her absence was particularly marked as Kathy ordinarily waited for her with dread; there was always something wrong with the food, something not hot enough, not cold enough, not fresh enough, or just not good enough, for the difficult actress.

After half an hour, Kathy returned to her office and placed a call through to Marcy's room. The telephone rang, but no one answered. She waited another twenty minutes in case the woman was in the shower, then tried again. Still no answer. A knock at the office door and the receptionist peered around. "Miss Devereux's car isn't in the carpark."

"What? Are you sure?" Marcy's gleaming maroon Jaguar hadn't moved for the last seven days, although it had been cleaned twice at her request. "Has Marlon taken it for valeting?" An outside guess as Marlon did all the valeting himself, priding himself on the professional finish he achieved.

"No. He said the last time he saw it was yesterday, before he left. He distinctly remembered because he'd spotted bird mess on the left passenger door and cleaned it off.

"Marcy didn't leave here last evening." Kathy had seen the woman make her way to bed after drinking hot chocolate in the drawing room. She had seemed radiant, a change that Kathy put down to her stay at Hemlock. "And I would have seen her leave this morning if she had come down." The thought that the car had been stolen crossed her mind. "Are any other cars missing?"

"I don't know."

"Please check."

The receptionist disappeared and Kathy tried the phone in Marcy's suite once more. Remembering that Marcy had called her agent to complain about her experience at the house, despite the ban, Kathy tried her mobile. It rang, but the actress didn't answer, and Kathy decided to call on the woman herself.

Nearly ten minutes later, Kathy stood outside Marcy's suite, the third since her arrival, and knocked. No answer. She knocked again, leaning an ear towards the door. With no response, Kathy tried the door knob. Unlocked, it opened to the aroma of Marcy's distinctive perfume. The bed had been slept in, but there was no sign of Marcy. Kathy checked the small sitting room. Again, empty. The only other room in the suite was the bathroom. With images of Marcy slumped in the bath, unconscious because of a fall, or even drowned, she called her name and nudged the door open with a tentative hand. Other than the towels and bathrobe dropped in a heap on the tiles, there was no sign of the actress.

"Where the hell are you?" Kathy whispered to the empty rooms. Pulling her mobile from her pocket she dialled Marcy's number again. Muffled ringing sounded in the room. "Damn!" Following the noise, Kathy stepped to the bed, spotting the charging cable first, and retrieved Marcy's phone. The screen read 'Miss Perfect'. Ignoring the insult, Kathy switched off her own phone. Marcy's stopped ringing. Fear began to eddy; she could not imagine Marcy Devereux leaving the house without her phone. She scanned the room, checking for the clothes that Marcy had been wearing yesterday. The violet, scoop neck, cashmere sweater and white capri pants worn whilst drinking her cocoa last night were laid across the long stool at the end of her bed. On the back of the door were two of Marcy's silken nightdresses both of which carried the house's laundry tags. There was no evidence of the nightdress she was wearing when Kathy saw the writing on the wall, the remainder being hung up inside the wardrobe. Marcy either got changed into another set of clothes, or left the house in her nightwear. A knot tightened in her belly. "Where are you, Marcy Devereux?"

Unwilling to alert Margaret Beulieu, Marcy's overbearing agent, or the police at this point, Kathy called Alexander, apologising for calling whilst he was unwell, and explained the situation. "I just can't understand why she would have left, but her car isn't here, and she appears – although I'm not sure – to have gone out in her nightwear!"

Alexander coughed, his voice nasal. "The last time I spoke to Marcy, she was extremely anxious. I perhaps shouldn't share this, although due to the crisis? She was very much disturbed by the hallucinations she had been having and was deeply concerned that she was going crazy, she also reported feeling numb - emotionally that is - and questioning her future. She was very bleak about that, called herself a 'has-been' and asked me what I thought of voluntary euthanasia, she even mentioned a clinic in Switzerland that carried it out and quoted their prices."

"Are you saying she was suicidal?"

Alexander coughed again. "Sorry! I'm full of cold—dosed up to the eyeballs though." He coughed then blew his nose. Kathy flinched at the noise piercing her ears. "Sorry, we were talking about Marcy. She didn't state that she wanted to kill herself, but she did say she was struggling to see the point in life."

"You've shocked me, Alexander. I would have said she was glowing with happiness last night."

"She is very up and down; neurotic, borderline manic depressive, I'd say."

Kathy flinched at Alexander's choice of words to describe Marcy's erratic behaviour. "Has she been diagnosed as bi-polar?"

"No, but you know how fragile these creative types are ..." Alexander coughed again. "It's just a thought, but would Marcy have a tracker on her car? If she does, then perhaps it's possible to trace her?"

"I hadn't thought of that-"

"Lots of the richer folk do, you know."

"... Yes, perhaps-"

"I would call the police. Let them deal with it."

Another cough and Alexander excused himself, leaving Kathy to attempt to process the situation; Marcy had been experiencing suicidal thoughts, had snuck out in the middle of the night, possibly dressed in her nightwear, leaving her phone behind. Kathy replaced the receiver, then dialled for the police.

CHAPTER TWENTY-ONE

The opaque clouds of yesterday's sky had thinned, and behind them was the promise of a bright day. Frankie ran down the steps at the back of the house, courtesy earplugs in, and tape player - a 1980s original that Kathy had to show her how to use - hooked onto the band of her running shorts, and crossed the wide expanse of lawn. Ahead lay a massive hedge of privet. An archway cut through its centre led to what Kathy described as a 'garden of rooms with places for quiet contemplation'. To the left was a maze, reconstructed following the late nineteenth century designs found in a drawer. To the right a walled kitchen garden led to an orchard. Beyond that lay the forest that Kathy was proud to tell her, covered ten hectares. Frankie headed to the forest, wanting to lose herself between the trees, although she decided to skirt the border as a precaution against getting lost.

A cassette of Beethoven's seventh symphony played on the vintage tape player as Frankie crossed the lawn, passed the walled garden, and the maze, then ran beneath the avenue of berry-laden holly trees to the back of the garden. The flowerbeds gave way to an area of open grassland and then the forest. Her feet already wet from the morning dew still clinging to the grass, she sprinted across the field, enjoying the surge of power, and push to reach her fastest speed, and arrived at the first tree out of breath. Hands up against its rough bark, she stopped, chest heaving, and looked back across at Hemlock House. It rose from behind the hedges and trees like a magnificent monster, its multiple windows black and shining eyes. The sun broke from behind a cloud, casting light across the building, and the eyes seemed to wink. With a laugh at her own silly thoughts, Frankie ran into the forest, relieved to be away from the huge but claustrophobic house.

Running between trees, delighting in jumping over worming roots, then jogging along paths worn by other 'guests', she remained near the forest's edge. After half an hour of skirting the edge, she took a turn to the right and ran deep into the forest. The land rose to a steep hill, and she grasped at saplings, roots, and trunks to help her move to its top. Rich soil pushed beneath her nails as she dug fingers into the earth. From the top, she ran down the steeper slope on the other side to the bottom where a shallow stream ran in the direction of the house. Through the trees, she spotted a brick wall. Moving closer, a derelict, single storey house came into view. The windows were shuttered, and a gaping hole sat at the corner of the roof where tiles had slipped, breaking the guttering in their fall.

Her watch beeped, an alarm to remind her of the beauty therapy session, brought forward in time due to the psychologist taking a few sick days. She increased her pace, leaving the house behind, but with the thought of returning to explore the area a little more tomorrow.

The hill declined, and Frankie followed its line, sure of reaching the edge of the forest in the next minutes. Movement in her peripheral vision caught her attention. A flash of crimson. A halo of bright yellow. A woman running through the trees! The figure disappeared as Frankie slowed to a heavy stop. Searching between thick trunks, she couldn't find the woman, but someone had definitely run through the trees. Chest heaving, hands on hips, Frankie walked forward keeping an eye out for the running figure. Several minutes passed without another sighting, and Frankie picked up her pace once more. A crimson flash in the corner of her eye. Again, she snapped her head to look. Nothing. A headache began to throb. Not here! Not in the woods! She was used to things moving at the corner of her vision, but that was inside, in her home, in the theatre, at Dean's office, but not in the middle of the woods. Last night's terrifying hallucination in the empty bedroom stabbed at her memory.

She pushed onwards, determined to talk to the psychologist as soon as he returned to work; coping alone with the fear that her mind was unravelling, and had become more than she could bear. She picked up her pace. At her back, footsteps pounded. In the next second, harsh breath rasped against her ear, and the woman in red ran by her side, shoulder to shoulder, arms pumping in unison. Frankie screamed, stumbled, then careened forward, arms wheeling. She landed with a thud as her ankle gave way. The woman in red, Marcy Devereux, disappeared behind a tree.

Frankie yelped in pain, then shouted, "Marcy!"

Marcy didn't answer, or reappear.

"Damn woman!" Pushing herself to stand on her good leg, Frankie tested the twisted ankle. It took the pressure quite well, although running back to the house was no longer an option. "Marcy!" she called. "Come out!" Marcy remained hidden and, irritated by the woman's stupid games, Frankie made her way back to the retreat, determined to confront the actress the next time she saw her. As she reached the edge of the forest, and the house appeared within its ring of trees, the image of Marcy sprinting refused to leave her. *What the heck was the woman doing running like a demented lunatic through the forest dressed in her nightie?* Frankie slowed. *She had a look of terror on her face too.* The image became clearer. *She was barefoot ... in her nightie ... without makeup!* Frankie took a look back into the forest; her mind was playing tricks on her once more—there was no way the uptight star, who wouldn't appear in her coffin without a full face of make-up, would run with a bare face through the woods, unless she's had a breakdown of sorts, and become lost!

Newly anxious for Marcy's safety, Frankie called the woman's name repeatedly before leaving the forest then limped, as fast as her injured ankle would allow, to alert the staff that Marcy was lost in the woods and needed their help.

CHAPTER TWENTY-TWO

As Frankie stumbled back across the field between the wood and the retreat's gardens, Kathy paced her office, discussing the situation with Evangeline.

"We should search the house and grounds."

"But if she's taken her car, then there's very little point in that," Kathy said with exasperation. It was typical of the egotistical actress to take off in such dramatic circumstances!

Evangeline chewed on her bottom lip. "You're right, but it just feels wrong to be doing nothing."

"We've alerted the police and her agent, I'm not sure what else we can do."

"Have you been able to check her mobile?"

"No, and to be honest, it goes against the grain to check through her messages."

"It does, but it could perhaps give us some clue as to where she has gone?"

"If she doesn't return, then I'll hand it over to the police—perhaps they can get beyond the password."

"Perhaps we're being overly dramatic. It's possible that she has just had a moment of ... upheaval ... and gone out for a drive in the car."

"That's what the police think, but without her phone, and in her nightdress? ... With Alexander saying that she'd had suicidal thoughts, we really have to cover all avenues. I just hope that he's wrong."

"I'm sure she'll turn up, Kathy," Evangeline placated although both women knew each feared the worst. "I'll take a walk through the grounds—just to see if there are any clues. Perhaps you could talk to the guests. I don't need to tell you to be discreet." Evangeline offered a weak smile.

"Do you know what I think, Eve?" Kathy didn't wait for an answer. "I think this is all a stunt. An effort by the egotistical woman to gain attention."

"Well-"

"It would be just typical of Marcy Devereux to pull a stunt like this, and if it gets into the papers, so much the better!"

"It won't come to that, and I'm sure that's not her intention. For one thing, it wouldn't go down very well with the production company. Her agent told me they were at pains to inform her that they didn't want gossip and negative press splashed all over the papers, given the role she is to play in the show."

Kathy deflated; she had begun to pin her hopes on Marcy's disappearance as being contrived, rather than the woman having fled the house in turmoil; if that news got out it could be very damaging to the retreat's reputation. "Well ..."

"I'm sure she will turn up soon," Evangeline repeated. "I must find Meredith or Peter and get an update on last night's vigil."

In all the commotion about Marcy, Kathy hadn't given the ghost hunting duo a thought. "They're at the B&B in the village. I did offer them the cottage for the time that they were here, but they insisted on staying there, and Peter was adamant about having access to reliable internet."

"That's understandable; it's hard being cut-off from the world once you're used to being so connected. I'll call them at the B&B, although it's possible they're still asleep after the vigil."

Evangeline disappeared through the door leaving Kathy to slump back down into her chair, the pain at the nape of her neck was becoming intense. The branch tapped again on her window. Already on tenterhooks, Kathy spun to the noise with heart palpitating, and screamed at the glass. In the window, for a split second, was the terrified face of Marcy Devereux.

The vision disappeared as quickly as it had appeared and, terrified, Kathy spun back to face her desk, pushed herself out of the chair, and ran to the door. With space between herself and the window, she took deep breaths to calm herself. *What the heck was the woman playing at scaring her like that!*

The phone rang as Kathy continued to stare out at the apple tree's autumn leaves nodding in the wind. The branch scratched against the glass. The phone continued to ring and, with heart thumping, she answered, listening to the policewoman as she introduced herself as Police Constable Helen Parsons. As the officer continued to speak, updating her about the search for Marcy's car, Kathy slumped onto the sofa; the tree, window, and face forgotten. Marcy's car had been found, and a teenage driver charged with theft. However, in his statement he insisted that he found the car beneath the Humber Bridge with the keys still in the ignition. The police officer promised to look through CCTV footage taken along the bridge on the previous night to search for any evidence of Marcy; a team of retrieval experts had been alerted to the case.

Kathy replaced the receiver, her mind numb, unable to fit the jigsaw of information together. Marcy's car had been found miles away beneath a bridge notorious for people jumping to their deaths from its drop of more than one hundred feet to the murky waters below. No one who had jumped from the bridge had ever survived, not intact at any rate; falling from that height would be the same as hitting concrete. But ... she had just seen Marcy's face at the window! Another tap on the glass. The hairs on Kathy's neck bristled, but it was only Marlon, tree loppers in hand, gesturing to the tree and then offering a thumbs up. In a stupor, Kathy returned a wave, then left her office to locate Evangeline and tell her the news.

CHAPTER TWENTY-THREE

As Kathy made her away across the elegant hallway in search of Evangeline, head reeling, Frankie reached the gardens of Hemlock House. The sprain in her ankle caused as she stumbled away from the vision of Marcy Devereux running beside her, had become increasingly sore and she hobbled past the maze, across the grass, and up the wide stone steps to the terrace at the back of the house before entering the drawing room. The room was empty, the only sound the ticking of the grandfather clock. A fire had already been lit in the wide fireplace taking the edge of cold from the room, but not the chill Frankie experienced as she stepped over the threshold.

With painful steps, she limped quickly, intending to go to the manager's office and tell Kathy, or whoever she found there, that Marcy was lost in the woods. The drawing room door opened into the large entrance hall and the silence of the room was replaced by excited voices speaking in conspiratorial tones. Alerted to the unusual and gossipy nature of their voices, Frankie hovered in the doorway, and listened.

"We're not supposed to know, but Marlon told me that they're looking for Marcy Devereux. They've found her car, but not her."

"I noticed it was gone this morning, but I thought maybe she'd checked out."

"Nope. And I heard Miss Fielding telling Mrs Maybank that they'd found the car beneath the bridge. Mrs Fielding looked sick, she was so white in the face."

"Which bridge?"

"The Humber Bridge! And ... the keys were still in it."

"No way! I know she was flighty-"

"She was a miserable cow!"

"Shh!" The other girl, looking around in case anyone had heard the other's coarse words, spotted Frankie. Her cheeks flushed. "Good morning, Miss D'Angelo." She spoke with a bright smile. "Did you enjoy your run?"

Frankie hobbled forward, attempting to hide her pain.

"You're hurt! I'll ask Sandra to come to you, she's our first aider."

"No, really, it's just a little sprain." Frankie reached the desk. She had to know exactly what they were talking about. "I couldn't help but overhear ... but did you say that Marcy Devereux is missing?"

The girl's eyes widened, and delight flickered in them. "Yes! Her car was found beneath the Humber Bridge. They think she's jumped. A helicopter's looking for her in the water, right now."

Frankie's knees weakened, and she gripped the side of the reception desk for support.

Alarmed, the girl made a quick move to stand beside her. "You're not alright. Let me help you to sit."

Gathering her senses, Frankie refused the help, insisting that she could stand and make her own way to her room, then pressed for more information.

"I don't know anything apart from what I've told you: Marcy is missing, and her car was found beneath the bridge. She left her phone here too."

Sickness swirled in Frankie's belly. If Marcy had jumped from the bridge, then Frankie can't possibly have seen her in the woods. She glanced at the closed door of the manager's office. If Marcy had jumped, telling management her story would make her look like a nutjob, or make them think she was stirring up trouble, and the look of contempt Neil had thrown her after the awful scene at the abbey, still made her want to curl up and hide beneath a rock.

CHAPTER TWENTY-FOUR

Police Constable Helen Parsons swung the car off the road and down the narrow track that led to Hemlock House. Her partner, Stuart Redwood, fingered the radio on his police issue vest. "... Negative. We're at the house now." He remained silent as the car travelled along the driveway, thickening trees cast the interior in shadow. The view brightened to opaque grey as they reached the clearing where the house stood.

"Bloody hell!"

His reaction matched her own – coming face to face with the infamous house was like a punch to the gut - and she pulled the car to slow in front of the imposing edifice then followed the discreet sign for the carpark.

"Bloody hell!" he repeated as they rolled over the gravel to the area of parked cars.

She fumbled for words, biting back emotion, and what she really wanted to say. "Impressive, isn't it."

He scanned the space. "There must be more than a million quid's worth of cars here."

Trust him to notice the cars! Though unimpressed by the array of expensive cars, Helen couldn't help feeling like the poor relation as she steered the Vauxhall Ford Fiesta police car between an immaculate burgundy Jaguar and a glossy black Range Rover.

"So," Stuart slammed his door shut, "this is where celebs come when they lose the plot?"

"It's a therapeutic retreat, but yeah, when they go off the deep end, they come here." Helen closed her own door with a gentler push.

"And Marcy Devereux, the woman allegedly missing, is an actress?"

"Yes, I've seen her in quite a few things. She hasn't been on telly so much recently though." As she continued to relay what she knew of Marcy's acting history, the door at the side of the house opened and an immaculately dressed redhead almost ran down the steps to meet them. The woman looked familiar.

Scanning her face whilst offering a smile, Helen was struck by the similarity between the woman, her grandmother, and another maternal aunt, although quite certain that she wasn't related. The woman proffered a hand then dropped it, suddenly uncertain of the correct etiquette. Used to the confusion, Helen held out her own.

The woman took it without smiling. "Kathy Fielding. I'm the business manager at Hemlock House."

"Morning, Mrs Fielding." Stuart's turn to shake hands.

The woman bristled with unease, and made no effort to take them into the house. Instead, with a glance at the police car, and then their uniforms, she said, "Can I ask you to be discreet please? Our guests are fragile, and in need of a calm environment. This kind of thing could set them back terribly. The tension in the house is already hanging by a thread!"

"We can only do our job Mrs Fielding," Stuart replied. Kathy darted him a worried glance and showed no sign of taking them inside.

Helen smoothed Stuart's rough edges, determined not to carry on their enquiries outside. "We'll make our best efforts not to upset them. Shall we talk somewhere more private?" She gestured to the man now crossing the carpark with a wheelbarrow.

With a small sigh, and failed effort to smile, Kathy relented, and turned to lead them into the house.

A tingling at the nape of her neck accompanied a queasy lurch as Helen crossed the threshold. She pushed away the emotion, silently berating herself for being 'silly', telling herself to be professional, but unable to quite shake the turmoil of entering the house of her Great Aunt Doretta's killer, the Fenland Ripper. Perhaps she should have asked PC Riddings to take this job, but the draw of seeing the house for the first time was irresistible. Yesterday morning the death of her aunt had only been a hazy footnote in her family's history; the pain of the event so dreadful to the girl's mother that it had become a taboo subject, buried over time, and it had only been a slip of her own mother's tongue several years ago, at the funeral of another great aunt, that the information had leaked back to the younger generation.

The business manager led them through a narrow, plainly decorated corridor that passed a busy kitchen, and then through to another corridor that opened into the reception hall. The place was a maze! It would have been so much easier to come in through the front door, but they had complied with the business manager's request of coming to the side. The manager paused at the door, presumably checking that there were no guests to see them, then led them at a brisk pace to her office, closing the door behind them with another sigh, obviously relieved, before sitting stiffly upright in her chair. She gestured for them to sit. After forcing herself to focus on the job, although hyper-aware of every surface in the room, Helen took out her notebook and pen.

The next ten minutes were spent asking questions about Marcy Devereux's activities during her time at the house, and her mental state. She had arrived at the retreat in an extremely anxious state, she was told, but over the ten days that she had been with them, her behaviour had become less erratic, her concentration levels far better, and she had taken to going for long walks in the grounds, swimming in the indoor pool, and had booked every massage, facial, pedicure, skin rejuvenation, and manicure session that it was possible to attend.

"Obviously, she was still … difficult, very demanding and picky about everything! But she seemed far more at peace with herself, and was elated that she had also lost weight, so I was dismayed when she started showing signs of distress once again."

Helen's interest aroused, she asked, "Can you explain what you mean by 'showing signs of distress', please?"

Kathy glanced at the wall beyond Helen's shoulder, took a breath, and explained the odd behaviour of the actress; how she had begun to seem nervous once more, and jumpy, and how she had called her agent to complain of seeing someone in her room. "It was night terrors, of course."

"Can you be sure it wasn't a real intruder?"

"The house is very secure, and Marlon – he's our groundskeeper and maintenance man – hasn't reported any signs of a break-in. We've been particularly careful since the owner's cottage was broken into."

"Did you report the break-in?"

"Yes." Kathy threw her a confused frown. "But I don't see what that has to do with this?"

"Just being thorough. Do you have the incident log number?"

"Yes, I do." Kathy turned to the stack of trays on her desk, pulled out a sheaf, then handed Helen a sheet with neatly written notes and the incident number printed at the top. Kathy was obviously a woman who liked absolute order and organisation. Helen noted the log number down.

"I'm positive they were night terrors. They stopped once we moved her to a different suite," Kathy explained. "She woke me up several times a night after they started, but Doctor Mansard suggested that I move her to a different suite and they stopped, and then she seemed to be her revived and bubbly self again. It was a complete shock to me when Doctor Mansard suggested that she was suicidal—I would have said quite the opposite."

"But she was up and down by the sound of it," Stuart added. "She wouldn't be here otherwise. This place is for celebrities with mental health problems, isn't it?"

"Well, I wouldn't quite put it that way. Our guests are often in the public eye ... we understand the pressures they're under ... the constant, often negative, scrutiny they have to endure-"

Stuart coughed, and Helen nudged his boot with her own. *Don't offend her, Stuart!* "We understand." Some of the tension dissipated. "And when was the last time *you* saw Miss Devereux?"

Kathy continued, explaining how the woman hadn't come down in the morning, which was unusual, and concerned her enough that she went to her room to make sure that she wasn't unwell.

"And you didn't hear anything unusual in the night?"

Kathy's eyes flickered and she visibly blanched, a phenomenon that Helen had witnessed before. The woman was remembering something and she would either lie, try to avoid giving her an answer, or make eye contact and tell the truth. "Unusual?"

Procrastination. Disappointing! Helen would have to dig a bit harder. "Yes, any unusual noises, the front door opening or closing, a car's engine, thudding, shouting?"

Helen watched Kathy closely, she hadn't reacted to the suggestion of the door opening, or the car's engine, but had flinched almost imperceptibly when she had mentioned 'thudding' and 'shouting'. The woman knew more than she was telling them.

"No ... Well, there has been a lot of thudding recently, which I had put down to Marcy's night terrors, perhaps her sleep walking, or one of the other guests being unable to sleep – they do come in with erratic sleep patterns, it's one of the problems we try to solve here, which is why it is so important to maintain a calm and healing atmosphere ..."

"You didn't hear anyone calling out then?"

A furrow between her brows then her eyes flitted to the wall. "No."

"Miss Fielding, is there something that you'd like to tell us?"

"Pardon?"

"Well, you seem a little on edge. I just thought that perhaps there was something you wanted to share, perhaps something that you're unsure of, something that you're worried will get someone into trouble?"

Stuart coughed.

Helen waited with interest for the answer, taking particular notice of Kathy's body language. The woman sat forward, grasped a pen on her desk. "I ..." Stuart leant forward too, noticing the woman's discomfort. "Well ... Now, this is going to sound very peculiar to you ... unless ... I'll just come right out and say it; I've had some odd 'experiences' in the last few days and the owner has insisted that we bring in some specialists to try and discover the source of the problem."

"I don't understand, Kathy. Could you be more specific, please?"

"I've had some ... what the owner thinks are ... supernatural experiences." A flush rose to her cheeks and she avoided making eye contact. "I'm sure that it's just stress and my overactive imagination, but Eve insisted." She dropped the pen, her hand visibly shaking.

Stuart's cough this time was more of a derisory snort. Helen kicked his boot a little harder.

A disbeliever, Helen was nevertheless intrigued by the unfolding story. "Supernatural experiences?"

Kathy's gaze flicked from Helen to Stuart, then back to Helen. Her cheeks burned red. "Yes, I know it sounds ... outlandish ... but I saw something in my room-"

Another man in a room at the house. "A man ... like the one in Marcy's room?"

"No! There was no man in Marcy's room. She didn't say it was a man – just a presence."

"What about the man in your room?"

"It wasn't a man—it was a woman."

"And did you recognise her?"

"No. It was too dark—she was just a shadowy presence."

"Then how do you know it was a woman?" Stuart asked.

"I ... I just knew. It's hard to explain."

"Is that the only 'supernatural experience'?"

"No." Kathy swallowed, her mouth obviously drying. For Helen, the spirit world didn't exist, ghosts, ghoulies, apparitions, the walking-dead, demons, witches, zombies, magic, none of it was real, but the woman's fear was. "This has nothing to do with Marcy's disappearance, but I saw something, or at least thought I saw something, in her room."

"On the night she disappeared?"

"No, it was the evening before that."

For the next minutes, Kathy explained her experience of hearing thudding then wails and sobs that she presumed had come from Marcy's suite. Unable to sleep, and concerned for the woman's emotional state, Kathy had gone to her room to check. Marcy had been asleep, but she had seen, or thought she had seen, names scribbled on the wall. The wailing voices had also spoken the names, and she'd been unable to get them out of her head.

"And are the names still there? On the wall?"

"No! That's just it. I thought that Marcy had scrawled them over the wall, but as soon as she realised someone was in the room and woke, they disappeared. It was all in my imagination."

"The names disappeared? So ... you had an hallucination?"

"Yes! Exactly."

"And why do you think that that was a 'supernatural experience'?"

"I'm not sure that I do. As I said, it was the owner who insisted on bringing in the ghost detectives."

Stuart failed to hide his snort of derision. Helen made no effort to kick his boot.

"And the names? Do you remember them?"

"Oh, yes. You see, that's why Eve was so insistent on getting help."

"And they are?"

"Barbara, Noelle, Mary, Doretta-"

"Doretta!"

"Yes, and the others were Annie, Betty, Doris, and ..." Kathy's eyes locked on Helen's, "Marcy."

"Doretta? Are you sure 'Doretta' was written on the wall?"

"Yes, it's such an unusual name. I can still see the vision now if I close my eyes; it seemed so real."

Unable to keep the burst of emotion down, Helen blurted, "What kind of sick, twisted games are you playing here!"

"Games? What!"

CHAPTER TWENTY-FIVE

It had taken only seconds for Helen to realise that she had overstepped the mark. The wash of offence that fell across the manager's face had been immediate, and she sat across from Helen with a stony face for several excruciating seconds. Surprisingly, it was Stuart who had smoothed the tension in the room, and within minutes the women were talking again, but this time with Helen stepping out of her official role.

An hour had passed since the meeting in the manager's office, and Helen stood in the foyer of the B&B where the ghost hunting detectives had rooms, unable to believe that she was even entertaining the idea that they were genuine. What was more likely, she thought, was that there was a scam afoot at Hemlock House. Quite what, she couldn't fathom; nothing added up.

"It's some sort of scam," Stuart said, echoing her thoughts. Stuart had barely spoken since leaving Hemlock House and chose his words carefully, tip-toeing around the grieving niece of a serial killer's victim.

"I didn't know her—my aunt Doretta. She died before I was born."

"Still ... it must have come as a shock ... to hear her name earlier."

"Massive!" Relieved at the break in tension, she continued. "I don't know what is going on at that house! How could she have known about my family?"

"I think that's just one of those bizarre coincidences."

Helen lost herself in thought for a moment. "... Do you think she's telling the truth?"

"I think she believes she saw something."

"Do you think they're real then?"

"What? Ghosts? No way. My mum and sister do—they go to see a medium and try and talk to my Dad-"

"But he died a few years ago."

"He did."

"Sorry, I didn't mean to be so insensitive."

"You weren't. The point is, they believe that his spirit is out there somewhere. Me? I just think the psychic is pulling a fast one and smiling as they hand over their twenty quid."

"Is that what they charge?"

"Apparently so."

"Can't be bad."

Stuart laughed. "I'd rather catch the scammers than be one."

"Me too."

The conversation dwindled as they continued to wait for Meredith Blaylock and Peter Marshall of Blaylock and Marshall Investigations to appear. The woman was the first down the stairs. After initial introductions, Helen led her across the dining room to the table furthest from the door, thankful that the room was empty.

"You may not be aware, but Marcy Devereux, a guest at Hemlock House has been reported missing."

"Oh? I'm familiar with the name, of course, and knew she was a guest, but not the woman, so I'm not sure that I can be of any help."

"We have reason to believe that she disappeared under suspicious circumstances."

"Oh!"

"Can you explain to us exactly what you were doing at the house last night?"

A tall figure appeared at the door, and a broad-shouldered, attractive man waved at Meredith, then strode towards them.

"Oh, Peter, I'm so glad that you're here. The police want to interview us in connection with Marcy Devereux's disappearance."

"Marcy Devereux has disappeared?"

"Yes, Mister Marshall. We have located her car."

"I don't understand. Why does that mean she is missing. Aren't people allowed to go out in their cars these days?"

"She left Hemlock House possibly dressed in her nightwear, without money, or her mobile phone. Her car was found with the keys still in the ignition many miles from the house. We haven't been able to locate her yet."

"Oh ... Well, how can we help you?"

"We'd like to know exactly what you were doing at the house last night. Mrs Fielding stated that you were carrying out a survey throughout the night. Perhaps you saw Marcy Devereux during that time?"

"Nope. We definitely didn't see Marcy Devereux."

"What kind of survey were you carrying out?"

Meredith bridled, sitting straighter in her chair. "We were carrying out an investigation into the supernatural occurrences at the house. The manager had reported seeing an apparition in her room, along with hearing voices wailing a particular string of names that she also saw written on the wall. The retreat's owner, Mrs Evangeline Maybank is sure that the house has become haunted ... by its past owner."

"The Fenland Ripper."

"Yes. That is correct. Marcy Devereux, we believe, has also been disturbed by its presence, although she is under the impression that she has experienced night terrors, a belief that we aren't ready to dispel."

"The names-"

"The names that were written on the wall, and which Kathy heard called, are those of the Ripper's victims."

"Apart from one."

"Pardon?"

"Marcy. Kathy Fielding stated that 'Marcy' was also written on the wall of Marcy Devereux's suite."

"That is correct."

"Well, didn't it occur to you that Marcy was the odd one out?"

"Well ..."

"And now she has disappeared in very odd circumstances."

Peter exchanged a glance with Meredith, both obviously processing their thoughts. "Are you saying that you think it was a premonition?"

"Not at all," Helen replied.

Stuart shook his head. "We don't believe in that stuff."

"What my colleague means is that when people disappear, there is usually a valid, purely mortal, if not illogical, reason for doing so. Do you think someone set out to scare Marcy? Perhaps drive her away from the house?"

"I have no idea!"

"She didn't even see the names. It was Kathy who experienced that phenomenon. Her account of the vision of writing was very detailed."

"We were called in to investigate a series of what is believed to be supernatural occurrences. Everything we have recorded so far has only reinforced that hypothesis."

"Recordings?"

"Yes, we carried out a vigil and took readings, images, and audio recordings."

"And did you find any ghosts?"

"We think so. I took notes, if you'd care to read them."

Ten minutes later, Helen sat engrossed in the notes taken down by Peter during the interview with Kathy Fielding. Unable to shake the belief that the woman was somehow involved in Marcy's disappearance, and carrying the dregs of offence that her aunt's horrific and tragic death was being exploited, she scoured the verbatim account. Fascinated by the details of their detective work the previous evening, she asked about the readings, who 'Frankie D'Angelo' was, and then returned to the scene in the bedroom. "She gives a very detailed description of the names, how they all differ slightly, how they appear to be written in different hands, the colour and pattern of the wallpaper-"

"Which is not the same as the wallpaper in the room Marcy Devereux was inhabiting."

Helen requested permission to take a photograph of Peter's notes regarding the room. He gave his consent, then said, "We think it's a vision of that particular room, or one of the other rooms in the house, before the present owner renovated it."

"You mean when Barry Putchinski was ... resident?"

"Yes, you do know that he killed many of his victims in that house?"

Helen nodded, the urge to share her connection overwhelming. "My aunt died there."

Silence fell among the group, and Helen was surprised at the emotion the confession brought. Meredith slipped an arm across her shoulder. Ordinarily she would pull the woman's arm away – it was unprofessional in her capacity as a police officer – but she allowed it to rest there, taking comfort from the woman's kindness.

"I could tell that you were in pain the moment I saw you."

"I feel silly! I never knew her. The family never spoke about what happened."

"And therein lies the pain—your family has suffered terribly because of Barry's crime."

Helen nodded. The sadness and horror of Doretta's cruel death had crept through the older generation like a canker. "My aunt's mother suffered the most. I thought she was an odd woman, but it was only after I discovered about the murder that my own mother explained how it had changed her; she never recovered. My mother blamed it on her going to court and hearing exactly what happened to her daughter—what Barry did."

Meredith sucked air between her teeth. "That would be a terrible burden to have to carry. I haven't read the case notes although I have spoken to the current owner who knew him-"

"She knew him!"

"Yes, she nursed him at the prison until he died. She told me that she'd read his biography and that the details haunted her still."

"Biography?"

"Apparently so. It's unpublished, written by another inmate, a eulogy rather than an account of his ... crimes, although it is detailed—quite graphic. There are photographs too, of the house whilst he lived there."

"Of the crimes?"

"She did confirm that."

"That is ... sick."

"It is."

Disturbed by the revelation of the book's existence, Helen rode back in silence to the police station, unable to shake the concern that Marcy's disappearance was somehow linked to the bizarre story being told about the house.

Still cynical about the psychic investigator's claims, but determined to find clues that would explain the events at Hemlock House and Marcy's disappearance, she logged onto the police station's computer system, and checked for information about Kathy Fielding, Evangeline Maybank, and Marcy Devereux, then began the search for the Fenland Ripper's original case notes.

The fourth cup of coffee had been the one to make her stomach swirl with nausea, but Helen was determined to read through Barry Putchinski's file. Scrolling through the coroner's reports, the psychiatrist's report, and the police interviews, she stopped at the first photograph but quickly continued, the image too graphic to stomach. Several images later she found the image she had hoped would be in the collection. A wall scrawled with names. She zoomed in. Written in crimson ink, in shaking, but different, hands, were the names of his victims: Barbara, Noelle, Mary, Doretta, Annie, Betty, and Doris. No

Marcy. Of course, no Marcy. She wasn't one of his victims. Her gaze returned to 'Doretta', written in a distinctive copper-plate hand so similar to her grandmother's. She scoured the slightly blurry and typewritten paragraph below the photograph in the distinctive font of a manual typewriter and read about how the signatures were confirmed as those of the victims. Like all serial killers, he had a particular modus operandi, and forcing the women to write their names upon the wall in the room where he ended their life was part of his; the signatures were his twisted collection of trophies.

She compared the account to Kathy's vision. Her description of the handwriting was the same as in the original photograph from the crime scene with the exception of Marcy Devereux's name. The wallpaper was also different to that described by Kathy. She scoured the newspaper accounts. Surprisingly little had been published about Barry's crimes, and the detail about the names written on the walls had been omitted from all reports. Helen sat back in her chair, took another nausea-inducing swig of coffee, and then smiled. Kathy Fielding was definitely up to no good, possibly alongside the owner who, Meredith and Peter had confirmed, had a detailed biography, complete with photographs, and who had inherited the house from Barry Putchinski himself. Making scribbled notes about her hypothesis, she printed off the image of the wallpaper, logged off, and made her way home, determined that first thing in the morning, if Marcy hadn't been found alive and well, she would report her concerns to her superior and suggest that a murder enquiry be launched. *Ghosts! Hah! What a load of rubbish.*

CHAPTER TWENTY-SIX

Ignoring the footsteps and thudding of the guests on the floor above hers, Kathy drifted into a light, but exhausted sleep. The day had been difficult, her nerves overstretched, and the tension in the house palpable. It had become quite obvious as the morning became afternoon, that news about Marcy's disappearance was a source of gossip among the staff, and the gossip had quickly leaked to the guests. Several of the women had broken down in tears. One particularly theatrical television host insisted they hold a vigil, and prayed for her soul. Another refused to attend as the vigil was 'supremacist' and 'divisive' as it included a prayer to a god she didn't believe in, and stropped off. Arguments then ensued, and the atmosphere in the drawing room had become poisonous, resulting in one actor insisting she be moved to a different floor as they could no longer 'suffer' their neighbour, who, she now realised, was an insufferable bigot, and whose snores could be heard through the 'paper thin' walls. The descent into dissatisfaction, and the consequent derogation of Hemlock House, was beyond Kathy's endurance, but she complied with the difficult guest's demands with a tight smile and her professional armour locked into place, and retired to bed with a headache bordering on a migraine.

Her dreams were distorted, running through her unconscious mind like an art-house film; broken images of Marcy at the house cut away to still shots of the Humber Bridge, to remembered moments of walking along its banks, and more than once she woke to a state of semi-consciousness where she was vaguely aware of a knocking or thudding, before sinking back down into a fitful oblivion.

As her digital bedside clock changed to '02:59' her bedroom door opened.

Aware of someone watching, Kathy awoke.

A black shape hovered, and the outline of a figure was discernible in the dark room.

Her startled eyes stared into its charcoaled hollows as it descended, and a hand stifled her scream.

CHAPTER TWENTY-SEVEN

After hobbling back to her suite, Frankie had collapsed on her bed, reliving the dreadful run through the forest. The bedroom had been warm, the fire replenished with logs, the first aider arriving to look at her ankle, and a tray with biscuits and a teapot filled with hot chocolate delivered. The comfort of the room, and the kindness of the staff, helped her to relax, and there had been no more hideous hallucinations, no shadows in her room, no flickers of movement in her peripheral vision. Her foot resting on a pillow, expertly bound in a crepe bandage, the fire burning in the hearth, and the hot chocolate warming her from the inside, she drifted into a delicious, desperately needed sleep that lasted throughout the afternoon, evening, and late into the night.

As the figure that had hovered over Kathy carried her from the house, Frankie awoke with a start to screaming. Heart hammering against her ribs, she listened to the scream as it faded to a wail, and then a moan, and then to silence. Skin creeping, she fumbled for the bedside lamp. Light forced back the dark to the corners of the room.

The wail rose again to a scream then trailed off to a moan. The noise seemed to melt into Frankie's bones. As it started up again, she covered her ears, but the noise filtered through. Whoever was making the noise needed help, even if they were only having a terrible nightmare. She threw off her covers, unable to stand the noise for another second.

Peter, the conservation guy, must have heard the noise this time! How could anyone not? After last night's embarrassment of talking to him dressed in her less than glamorous dressing gown, she quickly changed into jeans and jumper, freshened up and brushed her teeth, then hobbled her way to the floor where he had set up his equipment the previous night.

The wailing continued, an ebb and flow of moaning, that grated her very soul.

Ignoring the noise, desperate for confirmation that Peter could hear it too, she made her way up the stairs, seething at the pain in her foot. The corridor was dark. Peter was not there. The wailing started again, and this time words were sung within it. The voice undulated, a tendril of ice that wrapped around her senses. Where are you Peter?

At the next flight of stairs, she listened for any sound that could give her a clue to Peter's location. Above, footsteps padded, the floorboards creaking. She took the flight of stairs, stepping closer to the low moaning of wailing voices. The sounds were repetitive, the words oddly formed, indecipherable.

Torchlight blinded her as she reached the top riser. *Peter!* "Please tell me you can hear that!"

"Hear what?"

No! "The voices! The wailing. The skin-crawlingly awful moaning and crying!"

Torchlight shone into her face. She made an effort to shield her eyes. He lowered the torch with a 'sorry!' then listened. The voices continued to moan their song of pain.

"Nope. Can't hear anything."

"You're kidding. You've got to be kidding me!"

"No! I- ... Frankie, are you alright."

"Yes! No! Oh, my God! All I can hear is terrible wailing. It's filling my head." She gripped his sleeve. "But if you can't hear it, then … I'm … It's just in my head!"

"Stay calm. Sometimes other people hear what we can't …"

Head reeling with the noise and the disappointment that Peter still couldn't hear it, she noticed the camera on the tripod illuminated by a large torch shining up at the ceiling. Several bags sat beneath the tripod, cables snaked across the floor, disappearing into the room. A device was clutched in Peter's hand; a black box with small lights and a tuning knob. She recognised the device; her gut rolled. Taking a step closer, she also recognising the thermal camera at Peter's feet.

"I thought you were measuring damp!"

"Yes … there is some damp."

"It's the middle of the night!"

"Yes, well … we need to … lots to do … and we don't want to disturb the guests."

She recognised a hacked radio, then noticed the motion sensor. "What else are you measuring?"

The radio crackled and Peter flinched. She threw him a piercing look as her thoughts gathered. "I recognise some of your equipment …"

"Well …" The man fumbled with the wires, placing the black box back into the holdall at his feet. "We're just …"

Frankie stared at him with interest, waiting for the lie, fascinated to hear his excuse for being on the landing in the middle of the night with a bag full of gauges that no conservationist would use.

"Well …"

After his failed attempt at explanation, Frankie's patience snapped. "I recognise those, and that. And the camera too!" She glared at him as her suspicions grew. "Dean sent you didn't he! He's set me up! Oh ... my ... God! And that's what all the noise is about. Well! Of all the ... I know exactly what he's doing now, and you can tell him from me that he is no Ridley Scott!"

"What? Ridley Scott? I'm completely lost! I have no idea who Dean is. I'm here with Meredith. We're-" He faltered again, obviously biting back his words.

"I'm not interested in your lies! Dean is a lying, conniving snake who will do anything for ratings."

"I've already told you; I don't know who Dean is!"

"Then tell me the truth, or I'll call the police! You're obviously not a conservationist, or a guest."

"The police? No! There's no need to do that." Peter sighed, his face becoming serious. "Listen, you're right, I'm not a guest, not technically, but I am employed by the owner to-"

"Employed? Don't try the damp expert rubbish again!"

"No!" He fumbled with the device in his hand. "Well ... we are kind of here to conserve energy-"

"For heaven's sake, just stop! I know exactly what you're doing."

"You do?"

"Yes!" She pointed at the camera on the tripod. "That is a camera with a full spectrum lens, and that is a thermometer, and that is an EMF meter." She prodded an angry finger at each item. "And the only people I know who would have a kit containing that particular mix of items are ghost hunters."

The look of surprise on the man's face was almost comical, but the pain riding Frankie killed any mirth she might feel. "I'm right! Aren't I."

"Well ... yes."

"So, you are here for Dean! The conniving snake!"

"No! I don't know who Dean is."

"The director of *Ghost Hunter PI*, the show that I present, or did present."

"Oh!" Peter took another look at Frankie, shining the torch close to her face. "So, it is you!"

The wailing that had woken Frankie, and enveloped her in terror, began again. Peter made no reaction. Ignoring the noise as fakery, she pointed at the box in Peter's hand. "What's that?"

"It's a device that helps us to capture instances of EVP."

"Electronic voice phenomena?"

"Yes! We record throughout the night and then feed the recordings into the software. It searches for spikes and patterns that are redolent of speech."

"It doesn't work then!"

"Well, it's not switched on at the moment."

"Switch it on now and tell me what you hear."

Peter glanced about the corridor. "You can still hear noise?"

"Yes!"

"Well, I'd have to record it and then upload it to my translation software. We could listen to it together tomorrow."

"Sure! More lies."

"No! I have other recordings."

"Sure. I bet Dean loves those."

"Miss D'Angelo, I promise you that I don't know Dean, although I have watched *Ghost Hunter PI*—on occasion."

"Then you'll know it's a shed-load of lies!"

"Well ... it is pretty obvious the programme is fake—at least to anyone in the business."

Frankie's cheeks began to burn; *had she been the last to know it was all a con?*

Deflecting her growing embarrassment, she said, "You said you had a recording."

"Yes."

"So, you're telling me that you have a recording of a ghost talking?"

"Yes."

What a crock! "Then, can I listen?"

"I haven't taken any recordings here yet, but I can play something for you from another investigation."

"An actual spirit speaking?"

"Well, obviously the software translates for us, so it's not a recording of its actual voice. Think of it like the computer software Stephen Hawkins used."

"Sure."

"Would you like to hear? It is a little ... scary though."

Seriously! "Sure, as long as it's not too disturbing."

"Well, it does sound a little ... mechanical, but ... wait, I know just the one." Peter clicks at his keyboard, passing the earphones to Frankie, then began to play the recording. Frankie's ears filled with the rustle of white noise. "I can't hear anything."

"Give it a minute."

A manufactured voice began to speak in stilted words that she couldn't decipher. "I don't understand what it's saying."

Peter adjusted the tone and speed. The voice became clearer. Something began to speak with a lighter voice, perhaps female, and the hairs on Frankie's arm began to stand.

"Julie! ... Where ..." White noise. "... you? ..." More white noise. "... Hot ... too hot. It's too hot. Julie, help me!" The rush of crackling static. "It's burning! ... Julie!"

Pulling the headphones off with a jerk, she handed them back to Peter. His grin was triumphant. "Fantastic isn't it!"

"It's ... tragic. Is it a child do you think? It sounded so lost."

"Well we can't tell gender, or age, from the recording, but yes, that's exactly what we believe it to be; a young girl. She died in a fire at her home. The house we were called to had been built on the site. Meredith managed to convince the child to pass to the other side."

"I could hear her clearly ... the voice didn't sound mechanical."

Peter caught her gaze, searching her eyes, then rewound the clip and listened through the headphones. "It's mechanical to me—stilted and quite deep."

Frankie dry swallowed. "I heard a young girl." The hairs on her arms bristled. "Tomorrow, after you've taken your recordings tonight, can I listen to them?"

"Well, I may have to get permission from the owner ... and I'll have to talk it over with Meredith ... but I don't see why not."

Frankie nodded, unable to force a smile of thanks. "So, you believe in ... ghosts?"

"Absolutely."

The headache at the back of Frankie's head pounded, and cold descended from the top of her scalp to her toes in a rapid wave. She swayed, holding onto the wall for support. "And, have you seen any?" The wailing resumed, and Frankie covered her ears.

"Can you still hear the voices?"

"Yes."

Peter squatted, inserting a cable into his EVP recorder and switched it on.

CHAPTER TWENTY-EIGHT

Watching Peter organise ghost hunting equipment was in stark contrast to the efforts that were made by Dean, Jake, and Callum whilst filming for *Ghost Hunter PI*. Constantly checking the cables, adjusting the knobs, and monitoring the input, he walked up and down the corridor, and around the vacant room, taking readings with a variety of gauges.

"There's a definite drop in temperature here," he said pointing to a corner of the high-ceilinged room.

"This was Marcy Devereux's suite, right?"

"Yes, it was her second room. This is where Kathy Fielding had her first experience."

"What experience?"

"Well ... I don't mean to be rude, but that information is ... classified."

"Classified!" Frankie made a small laugh. "You make it sound like some sort of top-secret operation."

"Okay, bad choice of words." He turned to her then, his face dropping to serious. "You can hear voices that I can't."

"Maybe."

"I think you're sensitive to the spirit world."

Without waiting for a response, Peter continued to press, asking her if she sometimes saw shapes in the corner of her vision, or felt as though she were being watched. She wanted to open up to him, tell him everything, feel the relief of someone believing her, and washing away the fear that she was going mad, but now wasn't the time; she felt far too fragile, too vulnerable, to allow herself any hope. Instead of agreeing, she offered a guarded, self-preserving, "Perhaps".

"Well, I don't want to colour your experience tonight by telling you about Kathy's experience."

"In case it distorts my experience?"

"Exactly."

"Will you tell me tomorrow?"

Peter laughed. "You don't give up!"

"Nope." Despite standing in a dark room in the middle of the night with a ghost hunting detective, or perhaps because of it, Frankie felt more at ease than she had since stepping over the threshold of Hemlock House. "Did you feel ... strange ... when you first came into the house?"

"Strange? No. It's impressive, but I didn't get a sense of foreboding, or the chills, if that's what you mean. Obviously, because I was aware of some of its history, and because we were coming here to investigate paranormal disturbances, it coloured my experience – he smiled at the reference to their previous conversation – but I felt excitement more than anything. Meredith seemed a little more on edge, but-"

"I did!" Frankie blurted. "When I stepped through the door, it was like something unpleasant gripped me. I could feel its presence on my skin. The place is poisonous!"

"Wow! That's a strong reaction. Poisonous? Why did you stay then?"

"Because I thought it was just me, another overreaction, another sign I was going crazy." She bit her lip, her words instantly regretted.

Peter looked up from the gauge in his hand and shone the torch on the wall beside Frankie. Their eyes locked. "When we've finished here, I'd like you to talk to Meredith."

"Why?"

"Well ... I think she can help you."

"Oh."

He returned to the gauge and for the next minutes Frankie forced herself to focus on the equipment, and assist him in recording the milligauss and temperature in the room, noting down the nuances of drops and rises. "There's a slight change here," Frankie said as she noted the tiny increase in temperature in the corner of the room. "It's gone up a fraction!"

"That's probably the result of your body heat. The gauge is very sensitive and you've been hovering over it for a while."

"Sorry!"

"Don't apologise, it's fine."

Frankie took a step back, still watching the digital readout. The reading lowered. "I think you're right."

Peter grunted, and focussed on his EMF gauge.

"I wonder if perhaps we should just sit down, and be quiet? You seem to do a lot of moving around. Won't the ghosts be put off by that?"

"You sound like Meredith!" he laughed.

Relieved that he hadn't taken offence, Frankie took another step back from the temperature gauge whilst checking the reading. The numbers had dropped another degree. The reading changed again. This time it was two degrees lower; a reading that couldn't be explained by her stepping away. "Peter!" The numbers dropped again; this time another three degrees had been shaved of the temperature. "Peter!" The chill caught at her cheek, and was accompanied by the familiar sense of being watched. Taking quick steps to Peter, she stood close. "Peter, the thermometer has registered a five degree drop in the corner."

"The milligauss have made a massive increase."

Frankie gripped Peter's sleeve. "Is something here?" she whispered.

"The readings would indicate that. Can you still hear the voices?"

"Not at the moment."

"Grief!"

Alerted by the excitement in his voice, her nerves beginning to fray, Frankie asked a startled, "What is it?"

"The gauge! I've never seen a reading so high. And I can feel the drop in temperature, it's like an icy breeze!" He pulled away and Frankie loosened her grip, but followed him across the room; the last thing she wanted was to be alone, and even a few feet between them felt too far in this poisonous house.

Within thirty seconds, Peter had an array of cameras re-positioned to cover the room. "I wasn't prepared last night when the apparition arrived."

Apparition! Frankie tensed.

"But tonight, I'll catch it on film. I've got full-spectrum, and thermal cameras, and night vision, and we've got the audio."

"Can I help?"

Peter took a camera from his bag. "Sure. If you see anything, anything odd, take a photograph. Just click the button at the top—it's an automatic so you don't need to adjust anything."

As he spoke, Frankie took the camera. A light flashed in the hallway. "What was that?"

"My camera in the corridor. Something has tripped it," he whispered in an excited tone. "I've got a laser trip wire hooked up to a full-spectrum camera ..." His words faded as the voices begin again in earnest.

"Do you hear that?"

"That rasping sound?"

"No. The voices. The wailing has started again."

Peter took a quick step to the audio recorder. "The audio's on. Don't speak from now on."

The wailing undulated, words muffled, the singing out of sync, grating. Movement in her peripheral vision caught her attention and Frankie swung to it. Staring at the moving shape for a second, until she remembered the camera and clicked the button. The flash illuminated the room. Where there had been movement the space was empty. With more movement on the other side of the room, she tried again. This time something hovered in the lens as the aperture opened. She took another photograph, the flash illuminating the empty bed. The voices lowered to a whisper. She strained to hear, unable to make sense of the noise.

Beside her, gauge in hand, Peter said, "Readings are dropping." He stepped across the room, oblivious to the moving shape Frankie tracked with her lens. She took another photograph, illuminating Peter's back as he crouched to the thermometer. "Nope!" he sighed. The shadowy figure hovered beside him. An arm seemed to lift.

"Peter!"

The figure rose to full height.

"Peter!" The word scratched across Frankie's vocal chords.

"The temperature has gone up too. Did you capture anything on the ..."

With the camera gripped at her side, Peter's words faded as the light in the room grew intense. The rapid change from a dark space lit only by torchlight to an intense light as strong as any spotlight in the theatre, was painful to her eyes, and she made an effort to shield them from the glare. A putrid stench seeped into her nostrils.

"Frankie!"

The room receded as white light bleached out Peter's equipment, the carpet, the walls, the bed, and Peter's frowning face disappeared as the light engulfed him.

The voices renewed, starting as a low wheedle in her ears to a singsong. Still unable to discern the mingled voices, Frankie's head throbbed. The room had gone, Peter and his equipment had gone, and she was thrown back into last night's hallucination. The room grew dark until the only light was the dim glow from the bedside lamp. The lamplight disappeared and a hazy light grew from the centre of the bed to illuminate the woman at its centre. Just like last night, Marcy was spread-eagled on the bed in her crimson silk nightie, but this time thick leather wrist straps with sturdy brass buckles shackled her to the iron bedstead. The striped mattress of blue and cream ticking was stained. A name appeared on a wall marked by rings of damp, dark brown at their edges. In one corner of the room, the paper had begun to peel from the wall. As Frankie stood transfixed, invisible hands wrote shaking signatures in crimson ink across the paper's rosebuds and tendrils of ivy.

"Marcy!"

The woman writhed against the restraints. Her face contorted in agony.

"Marcy!"

A low wail filled the room.

"Doretta!" she hissed. "Annie! ... Ohhh, D-o-ris!"

The hairs bristled on Frankie's neck as Marcy continued to recite the names. With each name a signature appeared. This time, at the end of the line of names, 'Kathy' was written in a distinctive, shaking hand.

Marcy continued to writhe, bucking against the restraints, her voice high and wheedling. "Barbara," she hissed. "Noelle, Mary, Doretta ... Aaaa-nnie, Betty, Doris, Marcy ... Marcy ... Marcy .... Katheee!

"Marcy!"

For the first time, the writhing woman seemed to realise that Frankie was in the room and twisted to look. Stifling a gasp, Frankie stumbled back. As she reached the door, the light softened, Marcy's face faded, and the original room returned.

A hand pressed down on Frankie's shoulder and she yelped, stumbled back, and knocked past Peter. He grabbed an arm as she lost balance. Heart pounding, staring at the moonlit bed with its immaculate sheets and plump pillows, the putrid stench receded to be replaced by Marcy's distinctive, rather overpowering, perfume, and the writing on the wall faded then disappeared. The bed was empty.

CHAPTER TWENTY-NINE

Meredith poured a cup of tea for the actress carried into their improvised office by Peter minutes ago. He sat beside the woman as she perched at the end of the bed, a protective arm still around her shoulders. As she rested her head against his chest, Peter's aura sparkled with a dark excitement. The woman's aura was subdued, suffused at its inner edge with an intense purple that strengthened to black. Without staring, Meredith scanned the woman, recognising her as Frankie D'Angelo, the presenter Peter had spoken about with such distraction. Meredith handed the girl's tea to Peter, then waited for the intense black of her aura to recede and for her energy to settle. The black receded, but her energy remained fractious, and unsteady.

Moving to sit without support, the actress took another sip of sweetened tea, replacing the cup in the saucer with a trembling hand. Meredith had never experienced anyone quite like her; her energy was explosive, and the tension filled Meredith's senses. She suspected that the woman was a sensitive, some kind of empath perhaps. That her 'gift' was causing her great suffering was obvious.

Peter rose from the bed to stand beside Meredith, and both watched the girl. Catching their gaze, she offered a tentative smile. "I'm sorry ... I'm not usually such a flake."

Her discomfort obvious, Meredith nudged Peter and busied herself with the files stacked on a chair, packing a cable into a holdall, then asking for his help. Taking her hint, Peter packed two items into the bag before glancing once more at the emotionally fragile actress. Meredith straightened, there was no sense in putting off the questions that needed to be asked. Instructing Peter to retrieve the audio recorders from the suite, she waited for him to leave, then turned to Frankie.

"Can we speak openly for a few minutes ... before Peter returns?"

With a look of surprise, Frankie nodded an affirmative and shivered. Meredith placed a warm blanket around her shoulders and then asked, "How long have you been seeing spirits?"

"I don't!"

"Frankie, I feel sure that you do, and I can tell that it is causing you immense suffering."

The woman's shoulders sagged, and her eyes welled with tears. Her aura pulsed. "I thought I was going mad!" The words caught in her throat.

Despite the rush of motherly feeling, Meredith continued to question her in a brusque, though not harsh manner; over the years, she had found that being business-like often helped people talk without descending into floods of tears. "When did you start seeing them?"

She blushed. "It started ... with my first period."

"Which was?"

"When I was fifteen. I was a late starter."

"Interesting," commented Meredith, "but not entirely unusual. A woman's power often comes to the fore at that point, although we're so divorced from our true natures these days that many of us don't recognise it." Frankie's eyes widened as though with revelation. "Did you know that a witch's power kicks in at that age too, and is more powerful during the menstrual cycle, which as we know is so very often in tune with the lunar cycle?" Outside Peter's footsteps grew louder. Both women glanced at the door, then Meredith offered a broad smile, and in quieter tones said, "We must talk later, Frankie—you and I." Frankie's aura glowed around her slender frame.

"I'd love to."

"Now," Meredith said, as Peter opened the door, "dry your eyes and give me a stiff upper lip. You need to tell me exactly what you experienced upstairs—without becoming emotional."

• • • •

THE CHANGE IN FRANKIE as Peter re-entered the room was remarkable; she had transformed from a barely functioning, speechless wreck, to drying her eyes with a tissue supplied by Meredith, and asking to help set up the equipment with barely disguised excitement.

Peter gave Meredith a knowing glance. She raised her eyebrows with a quick smile in return. Her eyes glittered, and he knew that she would be desperate to talk to him about the evening later, dissecting each tiny detail. The table at the side of the room had been pulled to the centre, and two chairs placed around it, with the bed serving as a third seat. On the table sat the audio recorder, laptop, and ghost box. Cables linked the equipment and, once satisfied that everything was connected, he pressed the 'power' buttons on each device. The ghost box crackled as the laptop's screen came to life. He copied the audio recordings onto the laptop, then searched for the recording taken just before Frankie had her vision.

"This is the one we recorded in the suite. I couldn't hear anything, but Frankie is sure that there was a voice."

"Voices. There was more than one."

Peter pressed play. The ghost box crackled.

"Now this is where the ghost box app would help." He twisted a knob in an attempt to tune the hacked radio.

Meredith offered a sceptical, 'Perhaps, Peter,' as he continued to turn the dials. A high-pitched squeal erupted, piercing their eardrums.

"Ouch! Sorry." He continued to tune the radio.

"But I've done some research on those apps, and the community is very much divided. Rachel at Bertram Psychic Investigations said not to trust any ghost hunting apps. She said that using a mobile phone can create false positives."

"You can get false positives on any communication device. It has nothing to do with a mobile phone. It's how the user interprets the responses."

"I'm no expert, but doesn't a mobile phone send and receive a signal from a mast?" Frankie offered.

"It does."

"She has a point."

"Plus, most apps are for entertainment purposes and tap into your search engine on your phone and your contacts and anything else you have including any social media information. I wouldn't trust that kind of technology to 'listen' to ghosts."

"The ghost box is a communication device; we can attempt to speak to them too."

"Oh!"

"The spirit app I wanted to use sweeps a word bank and the spirit manipulates those words to use in communication. It's a step forward from the hacked radios. The word bank offers the spirit a voice."

"But does that mean we can't hear the spirit's real voice?"

"That's correct. We can't anyway, the ghost box doesn't deliver the spirit's real voice."

"But it did last night—the little girl on the recording. It was a child's voice I heard." Frankie's cheeks blushed as both Meredith and Peter stared. "I'm sorry ... I don't want to sound arrogant-"

"Not at all! We've just never come across anyone who can actually 'hear' the spirits when they communicate. I don't hear them, I kind of just sense them, and Peter ..."

"I can only hear what communications they attempt to make through the ghost box, which, as you've heard, is limited and robotic, although ... I guess you didn't hear that."

"Well ... it was at first, until you tuned it in."

The ghost box continued to squeal, spark, and 'rush' with static.

Peter turned another dial and the squealing receded. A low, but continuous noise emanated from the box.

Frankie sat up in her seat. "Can you hear that?"

"I can hear a noise, but nothing distinct."

"Names! At least, partial names."

"This is the beginning of the recording, where you were covering your ears."

Frankie continued to listen to the undulating whine. Tears welled in her eyes.

"Is it speaking to you?"

"It's the string of names I heard last night, and in Marcy's bedroom the night before."

Meredith reached for her pen and wrote 'Audio 5. Hemlock House' at the top of her notebook. "Can you tell us what they are."

"Yes."

"Peter, rewind it to the beginning. Frankie, please translate, verbatim."

Frankie wiped at tears with the back of her hand. Peter clicked play on the recording.

As the noise began, Frankie translated. "Barbara ... Noelle ... Mary ... Doretta ... Annie ... Betty ... Doris ... Marcy ... Barbara ... Noelle ... Mary ... Doretta ... Annie ... Betty ... Doris ... Marcy ... Kathy ... Kathy ... Kathy ... Ma ... Marcy ... Kath ... eee."

"Kathy!"

White noise returned and with it the undulating wail.

"Mary ... Betty ... Kathy ... Kathy ... Marcy ..." It's just the same string of names. "Should I continue."

"Let us know if it says anything different."

They continue to listen, Meredith with pen poised, until the recording ends.

"No, that's it. Only those names."

"And you're sure it was Kathy?"

"Yes."

"Her name was written on the wall in your vision."

"Troubling!" Meredith checks her watch. "Five am. It's too early to speak to the owner. I suggest we take a few hours rest and then take our findings to Evangeline, and alert Kathy too."

"Are you suggesting that this is some kind of warning, Meredith?"

"I'm not sure, but with Marcy missing in troubling circumstances, and now Kathy's name being included in the list, I'm not willing to take any chances."

• • • •

COLD STROKED AT EVERY inch of Kathy's skin as the draft blew across the room, her nightdress no protection from its icy touch.

CHAPTER THIRTY

Despite reading online accounts through much of the night, Helen awoke at five am. She had showered, and dressed, and sat at the kitchen table with her laptop open searching for any information about the Barry Putchinski case. The photograph of her aunt as a young woman, her hair a fashionably permed bob, her face elf-like, had caught her by surprise, and she had reeled in shock as she realised quite why Kathy Fielding had looked so familiar; she was an almost carbon copy of her aunt, minus the bob.

She printed the photograph off, and sat it on top of the photograph of the signed wallpaper, and made a packed lunch before calling in sick.

The journey to the house took more than an hour, the narrowing roads too winding and full of bends to be able to get up a reasonable speed. She arrived at the turnoff needing to stretch her legs and drink another cup of coffee, just as a black, mud-spattered Range Rover sped past, overtaking her as she was about to turn. She slammed on her brakes, avoiding the car by inches. "Arrogant pig!" If she had been on duty, she would have passed on his number plate to the traffic cops, but she was on personal business today. Too wound up by yesterday's revelations to follow protocol, she had determined to confront Kathy and Evangeline.

She followed the drive, and slowed at the point where trees gave way to a clearing and the vast edifice of Hemlock House was revealed. Magnificent against the overcast sky, it sat as a brooding monster, and a thrill of fear rode Helen as it stared back at her with blackened eyes. Unlike yesterday, the lights in the downstairs rooms had not been switched on, hiding the scenes within behind glass that reflected the dark sky.

Unlike yesterday, she pulled her car up to the front of the house, grabbing her folder from the passenger seat, and stepping up to the door. She pressed the bell, and waited. Minutes passed without anyone answering. She pressed again. Waited. Picked up the massive brass lion's head knocker, and rapped it against the doorplate. Footsteps grew louder and the door opened. The young girl who had sat at the receptionist's desk yesterday answered without a smile, her cheeks flushed.

"I've come to see Kathy Fielding."

The girl stared at her then said, "I'm sorry, but Kathy isn't here."

"Oh, then can I see the owner, Evangeline Maybank?"

"She's busy."

Helen threw the girl a frown. "I'm here on police business," she lied. "I'd like to see Mrs Maybank."

The door opened and the girl asked her to wait in the entrance hall without offering her a seat. Surprised at the lack of common courtesy, Helen remained in the hallway. As she waited, Peter Marshall and Meredith Blaylock appeared at the side door she had passed through yesterday.

Peter offered a nod of hello as he passed, then disappeared into the manager's office. It closed behind Meredith. *So, she is in! Why the lies?* With quiet steps, Helen stepped up to the door, hand raised as though to knock, and listened. The voices inside were muffled, but she discerned at least three. She knocked. Waited. When the door opened, she was surprised to see Evangeline Maybank at the manager's desk, her eyes puffy, her hair scraped back, obviously unbrushed. Meredith stood with her arm across the owner's shoulder. All three stared at Helen as though she was a particularly revolting bug caught beneath a glass tumbler.

Evangeline was the first to speak. "PC Parsons! We weren't expecting you. Who called you?"

Alert to the odd question, Helen repeated the question. "Called me?"

All four exchanged glances. Peter and Meredith were particularly guarded. Meredith's hand squeezed Eve's shoulder in a gesture that Helen took as meaning 'be careful what you say'.

Meredith was the next to speak. "Mrs Maybank has had some difficult news." Meredith took in the woman's casual clothes. "Are you here in an official capacity?" The woman's question held a tone of distrust, obviously on the alert since their conversation yesterday.

"Yes ... no ... I've been researching the case all night. I had to talk to you about what I discovered," she blurted, all efforts at coming across as the savvy police detective gone. "It's the handwriting. I've found photographs. I wanted to ask Kathy if they were the same as in her vision."

All three stared back at her in silence. This time Peter spoke. "I'm afraid Kathy isn't here."

"But her car's here, and ... she lives here, doesn't she?"

"Yes, she does."

"We can't find her! And ... there was another vision last night. The woman who saw it said that Kathy's name was written on the wall too!" Evangeline's voice verged on hysteria.

Helen's grip on the folder tightened. If Kathy wasn't here then she couldn't corroborate that the photograph was the same as the imagined scene. "Have you reported her missing?"

"No. I only discovered that she wasn't here before breakfast. I've had to take on her role this morning. I've barely had time to think."

"But you called back the investigators?"

"We've been here all night carrying out another vigil. We've just updated Evangeline on our findings and had no idea that Kathy was missing."

"It's too horrible!"

"Are you sure that she's missing? Surely, it's far too early to know that? If her car is here, then she can't be far."

"Her car is here, and so are all her personal effects." Evangeline held up Kathy's mobile phone. "I've checked her room, and it's as though she went to bed, and then just disappeared."

"Like Marcy did," Helen stated.

"Yes!" Evangeline sobbed. "Just like Marcy did."

"And just like the Fenland Ripper's victims did."

Evangeline gasped. "Yes!"

"That was one of the most disturbing elements of his modus operandi," Helen stated. "He was able to enter the victim's houses and steal them right out from under the noses of whoever else was in the house."

"He took great delight in that." Evangeline said, her face draining of emotion. "He lured them, groomed them first, they went willingly."

Startled at the revelation, Helen was reminded that Evangeline had read his biography. Her suspicions were aroused again. "That's another element of the cases that wasn't published Mrs Maybank. I've read everything I could find throughout the night. There's no mention of the handwriting either, but it was in the case notes. Was it in the biography too?"

Evangeline nodded then frowned. "You don't think I had anything to do with it, do you? You can't possibly ..." Her face drained of any remaining colour and she swayed in her seat.

Meredith's arm circled her shoulders once more. "I'm sure that she's not suggesting that," she soothed, then turned her attention on Helen. "Are you?"

Helen returned the gaze, eyes locking for uncomfortable seconds, but didn't deny the accusation. "There is something terribly wrong in this house."

Peter huffed. "Obviously!"

"Mrs Maybank. I'd like to see that book."

CHAPTER THIRTY-ONE

Thirty minutes after asking to see the book, Helen, Evangeline, Peter, and Meredith were working their way through the house to the attic where the book had been hidden more than ten years ago.

Meredith paused for breath at the top of the stairs, the sixth flight since they left Evangeline's office.

"One thing about this place," Peter said as he caught his breath. "It keeps you in shape."

"Kathy always says that. It's one of the reasons she loves working here."

"It is a beautiful house, Mrs Maybank."

"Thank you, Helen." All four stopped to rest. "I've done my best to restore it, but there are so many rooms that some have remained untouched."

"Since Barry Putchinski lived here?" Helen held Evangeline's gaze, a flicker of fear in her eyes.

"Yes, since Barry Putchinski lived here. I did cleanse it after I inherited it though."

"Cleansed?"

"Yes, a local ... I hesitate to call her a witch ... but I think she refers to herself as that. Anyway, a local lady came around and we went through each room with salt water, and burned sage. She also said prayers."

"Weren't you scared to live here?"

"At first, after my ... It was several years after Barry passed before I was able to live here. By then, the unease I'd felt had ... reduced, and after the witch had cleansed it, I didn't have any trouble getting to sleep at night, if that's what you mean." Peter swallowed. Meredith caught his gaze. Helen looked down the dark corridor with trepidation. "It doesn't do to follow one's imagination in this house," Evangeline added. "Afterall, it was Barry who committed the crimes, not the house."

All three nodded in agreement, although Meredith suspects more in order not to appear disagreeable than in truth. Houses could hold on to malicious energy, or rather it could infest the very bricks and mortar.

"Shall we?" Evangeline motioned to the corridor and the door at its end. The carpet was dusty with footprints. "Not far now and we'll be in the first attic."

"The first?"

"Yes, there are several, but I'm fairly sure this one is where I placed the book."

At the end of the corridor, the door opened to another corridor with a door at its middle. That door opened to a narrow staircase that wound steeply into the roof space. The smell of stale air was accompanied by dust that lifted to tickle Meredith's nose. As she sneezed, jolting forward, she noticed the footsteps imprinted into the dust. "Stop!"

The procession up the stairs came to a halt.

"Don't move."

"But, the book-"

"Look at the steps. Someone has been up here. There are footprints on the stairs ahead." All four scoured the stairs. Meredith's foot sat at the middle of a large boot print. "And did you notice the marks on the carpet in the corridor?"

"The footprints go up to the attic."

In silence the four ascended the steps, careful not to disturb the large boot prints. At the top, the room opened out into a vast space lit only by the grime-covered attic windows. Open beams, thick with dust, and hung with blackened spiders' webs, stretched overhead whilst the floor was laid with wide planks. Given the immaculate rooms downstairs, the attic was a surprise, a dishevelled mess of open boxes, strewn clothes, shoes, and chairs. Boot marks scuffed the floor, and imprinted themselves onto decades of dust.

"What a mess!" Evangeline exclaimed as she stared at the array of open boxes and drawers.

"Someone's been up here," Helen added. "And recently. These boot marks are fresh. This is the source of your thudding, not ghosts and ghoulies!"

"It looks like someone has been raving through it all."

"My uniform!"

Evangeline strode forward, grabbing a dress of blue cloth from the floor. The fabric was striped black where it had landed on the dust. The belt clinked against the floorboards.

"You were a nurse?" Helen asked.

"Yes, a mental health nurse."

"You nursed Barry Putchinski," Helen confirmed.

"I did."

"Which is why he left you the house?"

"Which is why he is tormenting me now."

"You think Barry did this?"

"Yes, I do! He's the one who has been thudding about in the house. He wants me out." Evangeline sobbed with the blue cloth screwed to a ball in her hands.

"Not unless Barry has risen from the grave. He's dead Mrs Maybank."

"I know he's dead, but ... he's alive too."

Helen shook her head. "Mrs Maybank, someone very much alive has been up here. I don't believe in ghosts, spirits, ghouls, or whatever you call them, but the man who came up these steps and rummaged through your belongings, is alive and well."

Evangeline continued to stare at Helen. "I saw him."

"When?"

"When he died."

Here is the truth, at last.

"His spirit rose from his body. It was hideous, truly hideous—so much evil ..."

Helen shook her head, her expression one of scathing disbelief.

"I thought the ground would open up and demons would take him to hell—that's where he belongs ..." She looked around the empty space as though checking he wasn't listening. "But it didn't, and he rose up, and disappeared through the window. At first, I thought he'd start to haunt me, but nothing happened, and when he left me the house, I was sure he would, but again, nothing ... until now."

"Mrs Maybank, this is the work of a living man, not a ghost," Helen repeated.

"I have to agree with Helen, Evangeline. Whoever has been up here is a living being. Spirits may move things, but they don't leave footprints, not these kind at any rate."

Despair lifted from Evangeline's face as she listened to Meredith speak, her aura thin, the edge that circumscribed her outline a dark purple fading to a weak lilac, and the energy she exuded crackled with suffering.

"Someone has been up here looking for something. Can you see if anything is missing?"

Evangeline shook her head. "I can't remember half of what I put in here, plus there were items that had been here for generations." She gestured to the iron-work day bed leaning against a wall, and the nineteenth-century rocking horse thick with dust. "Much of it had belonged to the Putchinski family. They bought the house back in 1898."

"Personally, I think this explains all the thudding in the night."

"It's very possible," Peter agreed.

"I bet if we check the other attics, we'll find the same foot-prints and mess."

"I think you're right."

"And, I wouldn't be surprised if this ..." Helen gestured to the mess of clothes and broken boxes, "is connected to the break-in at your cottage, Mrs Maybank."

Evangeline dropped her nurse's uniform back in its box and scooped up some of the other items from the floor. Dust ed-died and whirled.

"Is the book still here?"

Without speaking, she moved across to the wide chimney breast that sat at the centre of the wall. She removed several bricks, reached inside, and pulled out a package wrapped in cloth. "Yes, it is," she replied holding up the parcel.

CHAPTER THIRTY-TWO

Back in the comfort of her office, Evangeline sat with the book on her lap, still wrapped in the dirty tea towel. "It's a handwritten account, so not a published book, but one written at the request of Barry who supplied much of the information and ... details. There are photographs too ... I have to warn you, it is graphic, and disturbing. At the time, given my interest in mental health, I found it a fascinating insight, not only into Barry's motivations as a serial killer, but also into the psyche of someone who had pretentions to be one. The author, Seth Golding, was also a serial killer, but one who prided himself in copying other murderers. It's a biography that illuminates two characters, really. The words on its pages have never left me."

"How did you end up with it, Mrs Maybank? Did you inherit from Barry too?"

"No. He gave it to me to read whilst he was a patient of mine. After I'd read it, I could never look him in the face again ... He asked me to keep it safe, and never give it back to Seth Golding who wanted to publish it and, he thought, tarnish Barry's name. The men had fallen out at this point. I was to guard it with my life. I promised to do that, although more out of fear than any real intention of guarding it with my actual life."

"You've guarded it all this time. Barry wouldn't have cause to take umbrage about that," Meredith placated.

Evangeline threw the psychic a thankful glance. "True, but then why is he here?"

"There's no evidence that he is, Mrs Maybank," Peter added. "The recording that we have is of women's voices, according to Frankie."

"Yes, and Kathy reported seeing a woman in her room. Her vision in Marcy's room was of women's names on a wall."

"And Frankie corroborated those names with her own vision."

"Which mirrored Kathy's."

Helen scoffed. "Are you saying that the two women experienced the same vision?"

"Yes, that's exactly what we are saying, and when Frankie had her vision, she was completely unaware of how Kathy's had presented itself. She was very precise, the details of the vision were identical, down to the pattern of wallpaper on the wall."

"There was one important exception, though. In Frankie's vision, as in the audio recording taken last night, Kathy's name had been added," Meredith explained.

Helen continued to stare at Meredith as she spoke, disbelief flickered with confusion and then uncertainty.

"Are you suggesting that it was a warning?"

"Yes, given that Kathy is also now missing!"

"And Barry's modus operandi was to take his victims right from under their families' noses."

"It can't be Barry!" Helen said with exasperation. "He's dead!" The policewoman stared at Meredith and then Evangeline with disbelief. "I'll prove that it's not. I'd like to speak to Frankie D'Angelo."

••••

EVANGELINE OPENED THE book with hands that trembled. "I haven't read this book since before Barry died. Much of it is similar to what was printed in the newspapers at the time, although, given that it was a first-hand account ..." The book's outer leaf fell to the desk. The lined paper was filled with a neat, very small hand written in pencil.

"The Life of Barry Putchinski: Serial Killer' was written across the top. Centred below, in rather childish style, was written, "By Seth Golding'.

"Seth is the biographer?"

"That is correct."

"And he was also a serial killer?"

"Yes, but not as successful as Barry."

"Successful?"

"I just mean that he killed a lot of women over many years."

"And Seth didn't?"

"No, he only managed four before he was caught, although he bragged about killing many more—he details them in this book, comparing himself to other serial killers. He was what you'd call a copy-cat killer."

"Interesting."

"It is, although deeply disturbing. I found the style the book was written in very troubling. Seth obviously held Barry in high regard, called him a mentor, and even refers to him as a master craftsman at several points."

"So, he admired Barry's 'work'."

"Very much so, although Seth's true heroes were Jeffrey Dahmer and Hannibal Lecter."

An 'ugh' from Helen.

"Hannibal the Cannibal? But he's a fictitious character."

"I know, but no one could ever get that truth through to Seth."

Evangeline turned another page. "I'm sorry, but I really can't read this book. Just touching it is unsettling."

"I'd like to see the photographs."

Surprised at the determination in Helen's voice, Evangeline said, "I would have to advise against that."

"I've seen the original case notes, read the coroner's reports, seen the police photographs ..."

"If you're sure!"

"I'm sure."

Evangeline moved away from the desk. "Then please, look through for yourself."

Meredith moved beside Helen as she sat at the desk. "Are you looking for anything in particular?"

"I am." Placing the folder she had been clutching since entering the house on the desk, she removed the photocopy of the photograph taken at the crime scene depicting the names scrawled across the wall. "Take a close look. Do you notice anything?" She waited for Meredith and then Peter to look at the photograph.

"The names are the same as the ones from Kathy's vision! And Frankie's."

"They are, but that's not what I meant."

"Then?"

"Well, the names of Marcy and Kathy are missing."

"Yes, but that's not the difference."

Peter peered down, but shook his head. Pleased that her observational skills were superior, Helen pointed a finger at the wallpaper. "It's not the same."

"The wallpaper is different? What does that signify?" Peter's tone was dismissive.

"It means that Kathy and Frankie are just repeating the same story, trying to make it seem like a vision of the crime scene, when it's not."

"Which means?"

"She thinks they're in on it together," Meredith sighed.

Helen smiled. "Exactly, and I just bet this book has a similar photograph which Mrs Maybank hasn't seen in years."

"You're suggesting that this is a story concocted by Evangeline?"

"Well-"

"Ridiculous!"

"Is it?"

"I haven't concocted anything! I can't even remember what is in the book."

"Although you said that reading it, and I quote, 'had never left you'!"

Three pairs of eyes stared down at Helen as she began to leaf through the book.

• • • •

AS PC PARSONS SLOWLY turned the pages of the serial killer's biography, the tension in the room overwhelming, Peter left the office to fetch Frankie. Helen's words repeated in his mind, belief in the veracity of Frankie's vision was now sown with seeds of doubt; she was an actress after all.

CHAPTER THIRTY-THREE

As Peter knocked on Frankie's bedroom door, Kathy awoke from a chemically induced sleep to the thumping of footsteps over bare floorboards, and a mouth filled with rough cloth. Unable to comprehend where she was, she slipped back into the dark of oblivion, only to surface minutes later. Laying completely still, she forced her mind to think through the chemical fug that gripped it.

Cold stroked at her skin, and goose bumps decorated every inch of her flesh. Minutes passed and she became aware of pain in her arms. She pulled at them, but they remained locked in place above her head. Her fingers uncurled, and touched metal. She yanked her arms, the rope around her wrists chafed her skin. She attempted to shout, but her mouth only filled with a muffled grunt. The cloth too tight around her head, she was unable to open her eyes. Wood creaked as someone stepped onto the stairs. Footsteps grew louder until she heard the breath of someone in the room. She remained absolutely still. Heart beating hard. A cold finger stroked the bare skin along her underarm. She screamed. The man chuckled. Hot breath brushed against her cheek and warm lips pressed against hers.

CHAPTER THIRTY-FOUR

The night had taken its toll on Frankie and she had woken to heavy knocking at her bedroom door with a struggle to comprehend where the noise was coming from and a head so heavy that she could barely raise it from her pillow. It was only when the rapping had become insistent, angry almost, that she had realised someone was knocking. She opened the door to Peter's stern face. He didn't smile as he greeted her. After an indiscernible flicker of emotion in his eyes as they caught hers, he looked away. Wrapped in her fleecy dressing gown, Frankie remained behind the door. The moment was awkward.

"You're wanted downstairs." His tone was formal.

The difference in his demeanour from just a few hours ago, was huge; he had been so kind last night. Now, stiff and reserved, he was unable to meet her eyes.

"Is everything alright?"

"PC Parsons is here. She wants to speak to you about last night—the vision you had."

Peter continued to look anywhere but at Frankie. Nothing had changed in the few hours since they last spoke so it could only be that she was in her nightwear that was making him uncomfortable. *He's angry with you ... He doesn't like you ...* She pushed away her paranoid thoughts, and replied in a lighter tone. "Sounds serious!" She attempted a smile.

"Yes, I think it is." Their eyes locked for a second, then his returned to looking down the hallway.

"Have I at least got time to shower and dress?"

"Yes! Yes, of course." Flustered now, Frankie assumed that it must be her state of undress that was making him uncomfortable. She allowed herself an inner smile, ignoring the flow of negativity beginning to nag at her – *there's something wrong ... he doesn't like you ... he's angry with you ... No! He's just a gentleman who is embarrassed to see you in your nightwear. Who wouldn't be embarrassed for you in that fluffy, pink monstrosity of a dressing gown? You're lucky he hasn't laughed.* She took a breath, attempting another smile that died on her face as he offered a curt, "We'll be in Evangeline's office when you're ready. Please don't be long."

Unable to restrain herself, she asked, "Peter ... what is wrong? You're so different."

His eyes locked to hers. "Kathy is missing."

Kathy is missing as well as Marcy! Her tension eased; *it's not her he's angry with.* "I'll be down as soon as I'm dressed."

It took Frankie a record three minutes to shower, and another two to dress. Hair scraped back in a tight ponytail, face bare of makeup, she pulled on jeans, jumper, and walking boots, and grabbed her coat; ready to start the search for Kathy.

Her quick rap at Evangeline's door was answered by 'Come in' and Peter opening the door. Four pairs of eyes stared at her as she stood in the doorway. The tension in the room seemed to bristle as she stepped in, and she was immediately aware of being scrutinised, judged. Used to being the centre of attention on stage, or front of camera, she allowed the façade of calm-and-collected-Frankie to slip down over her; it was a relief not to feel so raw.

"You sent for me?"

PC Parson's gaze was unsettlingly piercing as Frankie walked across to the group at the desk. Peter stood with arms folded. Meredith stood behind Evangeline who sat at the desk, eyes red-rimmed, dabbing at her cheek with a tissue. Frankie swallowed. "Peter said that Kathy is missing. How can I help?" Frankie's heart beat rapidly against her sternum; the tension in the room scratched at her.

"We want to talk to you about your vision last night."

"My vision? But Kathy is missing. Aren't you going to look for her?"

"We are, but we need to speak to you first."

"The police have been informed, Frankie. They won't do anything until she has been missing for forty-eight hours."

"But they're looking for Marcy!"

"Yes, but that's only because she's considered emotionally unstable, and her car was found beneath a bridge."

"You think she killed herself?"

"It's possible, but we're hoping that she will be found alive and well. Back to the vision, Miss D'Angelo." PC Parson's eyes stared into her own. "Take a seat, please."

"I don't know how this is going to help Kathy, but sure, ask away." Her tone had been too defensive. PC Parson's eyes narrowed for a second. Frankie recoiled. Peter was also watching her from Meredith's side. Only the older woman cast a gentle look her way.

The next minutes were spent reliving the ordeal from last night, with PC Parsons being particularly interested in the description of the room in her vision. "It was a wrought iron bedstead, black. The mattress was stained, blue and white ticking, you know the kind like a cotton canvas with the little bits of string making dimples-"

"Could you see the wallpaper?"

"Yes. It was stained and had a pattern of pink rosebuds and ivy."

"And you say it was Marcy on the bed."

"Yes. The woman tied to the bed looked just like Marcy. She was wearing a silky, dark red nightie with cream lace."

PC Parsons removed the leather-bound journal from Evangeline's desk and opened it at one of the bookmarked pages. Removing the slip of torn paper, she held it open. "Or was it this woman?"

A woman, remarkably similar in looks to Marcy Devereux stared back at her. An old photograph, stilted and posed. "She's very similar, but no. I'm sure it was Marcy I saw. She was wearing the same red silk nightie I saw Marcy in ..." She faltered; the same red nightie she had seen Marcy wearing as she had run through the woods.

PC Parsons turned to another bookmarked page. "And did the room look like this?"

Two photographs were glued to the page. The first one showed the writing on the wall. The other a wider shot of the bedroom. Glued to the images, Frankie's mind reeled. The writing was exactly the same as in her vision, the same shaky hands, one a distinctive copper-plate script. She focused on the image of the bedroom, the wall in particular. The wallpaper was not the same. "The writing is exactly the same as in my vision, but the wallpaper is different. What is that book?"

"It's the biography of the Fenland Ripper, Barry Putchinski, the previous owner of Hemlock House. It's a detailed account of his victims, written by fellow serial killer Seth Golding." The police officer turned to another photograph. Frankie recognised the room immediately.

"That's it!" The image, a bedroom with the usual clutter of paraphernalia and a neatly made bed, complete with an old-fashioned eiderdown bedspread, was her vision reflected back at her. "It's the same wallpaper and there's the iron bedstead, but when I saw it last night, there was just a dirty mattress on it."

A smile, more of a smirk, had curled onto PC Parson's lips. Frankie recoiled from the scathing flicker in her eyes, and caught Peter's frown.

"Have I said something wrong?"

"Not at all, Miss D'Angelo. But I would like to know when you had access to this book."

"I've never seen it before!"

"Are you sure-"

"Of course, I'm sure!"

PC Parsons leant out from the desk, scanning her feet. Another smirk. "What size shoe do you take?"

"My shoe size?"

"Boot size."

"Well, the same as my shoe size! An eight."

"Big for a woman."

"What!"

Confused at the line of questioning, Frankie turned to Peter and was met with eyes that reminded her of Neil at the abbey. Something snapped. "You're saying that I'm lying, aren't you! Peter? Meredith?" They made no response other than pained frowns. "What is going on here?" No longer able to sit, the urge to run from the room immense, she stood. "What exactly are you accusing me of?" The tension within her exploded to a deep and unbearable pain; she had been accepted last night - Peter and Meredith had accepted her - and the years of anguish at the hallucinations she suffered had been washed away. The heavy weight of despair and anxiety crashed back at her like a wrecking ball and she recoiled from their stares, turned on her heels, and ran from the room.

The house is poisonous! Running across the entrance hall, Frankie made her way through to the back of the house. *They are poisonous!* She ran down the terrace steps, out across the lawns, past the maze, and into the woods. *You are poisonous!*

CHAPTER THIRTY-FIVE

The man left the room after kissing her lips, and Kathy listened as he went downstairs and opened the front door, closing it with a click. The click was followed by the distinctive noise of a padlock being locked into place. Footsteps followed, and then a car's engine thrummed into life several minutes later. Listening to the car shift into gear and pull away from the house, she tugged at her arms. Pain burned her skin. She writhed against the constraints, but the rope was tied too tightly around her wrists. Unable to loosen them, she pushed at the blindfold with her arm. It shifted, and grey light filtered through. She managed to dislodge the cloth, allowing enough space to see the room. On the wall, pink rosebuds and tendrils of ivy were marked by rings of damp, dark brown at their edges. In crimson ink, a name was scrawled in a distinctive, shaking hand, 'Marcy'. She tilted her head and saw a mass of yellow curls, matted and bloodied. *Marcy!* A scream, muffled by the cloth filling her mouth, erupted from her belly; that Marcy was no longer alive, was obvious.

CHAPTER THIRTY-SIX

As Frankie reached the treeline she slowed, her breath coming hard, a stitch stabbing at her side. Rage overwhelmed her and tears flowed. She leant up against a tree, glanced back at the house with a twist of pain in her guts, then stared back into the forest. The last time she had been here, she had run from the woods and back to the house, sure that Marcy was lost. With her car being found miles away, Frankie had become convinced that the sighting was just another one of her stress-induced hallucinations.

The vision was real Frankie!

The wallpaper wasn't the same as the one scrawled with names.

It wasn't the murder scene at the house.

It was the murder scene somewhere else.

You saw Marcy running through the woods—after she disappeared. You saw Marcy tied to a bed, in a room scrawled with names.

Frankie slowed, her thoughts whirling.

You saw a murder scene.

Marcy is dead!

You saw Kathy's name on the wall!

She slowed to a stop. Is Kathy dead too?

As she slowed, she recognised the broken stump of a tree. The last time she had passed it, Marcy had appeared running between the trees. *You see ghosts, Frankie. Visions of dead people. Meredith knows it. Peter knows it.* Ignoring the nagging thoughts, she retraced her steps, drawn to the dilapidated house. A flash of red made her stumble, and she stopped. Another flash between the trees and the running figure of Marcy Devereux appeared, dressed in the same red nightie as before, the same red nightie as in her vision. *Marcy is dead, Frankie.* Rooted to the spot, she watched the figure disappear through the trees, the woman's physical presence seemed thinner, opaque, the trees visible through her transparent form.

Frankie followed the apparition.

With glimpses of red as the spectre hovered between the trees Frankie was led to the broken house. Old and forgotten, with ivy snaking up its walls and into its collapsing roof, and moss clumping in its rotting window frames, the cottage stood grotesque.

She tried the door. It didn't move, obviously locked or stuck solid with rust. She made her way to the side of the house where the forest opened up to a cleared space behind the house and a rutted track led from an open gate. The track was rutted with tyre prints. Ivy and ferns lay crushed and drowned. The tyre tracks were fresh.

The side door opened to a small kitchen. A clean, bright blue flask sat on the counter among the debris of dust, dead flies, and flaking paint. Muddy tracks led across the floor to an inner door.

She followed them.

Through the door was a staircase. The dirty boot prints tracked up the stairs. With a tentative step on the first, creaking riser, she stopped to listen. Somewhere in the house something moved. At the top of the landing, she stopped again to listen. Metal creaked from behind a door.

In the distance a car's engine thrummed.

There were two doors on the landing. She opened the first to an old-fashioned bathroom, greened with moss, its white sink and bath greyed with dust. Above the window, the ceiling had collapsed, the walls brown with water stains. A shower curtain hung half-ripped from its pole, blackened with mould.

She listened to the noise from behind the final door.

Oblivious to the car turning off the road and onto the track leading to the cottage, she opened the door.

Inside was the room from her vision, complete with ironwork bedsteads and the damp-mottled wallpaper of rosebuds and ivy. She recognised Marcy's name scrawled across the wall. Beside it was written 'Kathy'. Frankie stifled a scream and turned from the sight of Marcy Devereux's body on one of the beds. On the other bed a body lay beneath a sheet, only its shackled hands and feet visible. Frankie pulled back the sheet. "Kathy!"

Outside, a car's door slammed shut.

CHAPTER THIRTY-SEVEN

As Frankie had run from the door, Peter had followed, but lost her in the labyrinth of corridors and rooms. A search of the house, and her suite of rooms, proved futile, and she was nowhere to be found in the gardens. He returned to the uncomfortable tension of the manager's office. "I can't find her anywhere!" he said as he strode back through the door. Only Meredith gave him a glance. Helen Parsons stood directly in front of Evangeline, and the woman seemed to be shrivelling beneath the policewoman's gaze. Beside her, Meredith's eyes were locked onto Helen.

"I'll be filing a report of my findings-"

Meredith bristled, her lips thinning. "Shut up about your findings!" Helen and Evangeline physically jerked at Meredith's outburst, and Peter watched as the woman, usually so patient, rounded on the police officer. "Frankie D'Angelo is a very perceptive, gentle soul, completely tortured by her own gifts. She had nothing to do with Kathy's disappearance, or Marcy's, and I absolutely believe that the first time she set eyes on either of them, or Evangeline Maybank, or this house, was when she first arrived."

"But the visions tell a different story. Both women had visions that were incorrect. Their visions may have corroborated, but they made the mistake about the wallpaper."

"Which means?"

"Which means that someone who had access to this book," she glared at Evangeline, "misremembered the details when she was coaching them-"

"You are so wrong, it is pitiful!" Meredith's tone was scathing. "Those visions were a warning from the spirits that inhabit this house. And," she turned to Evangeline, "those spirits are not Barry Putchinski." She managed a smile for the distressed owner.

"Then who are they?" Helen's tone was unapologetic, bullying.

"They're his victims. The poor women who died in this house, and, PC Parsons," Meredith's face grew stern, "one could even be your aunt."

"How dare you! How dare you exploit my family's suffering for this ... con!"

As Peter watched the policewoman rile against Meredith, and Evangeline sink further back into her chair, Helen's words repeated in his mind, 'they misremembered the crime scene'. The confusion of the past days cleared. "They didn't misremember the crime scene," he muttered. The women continued to argue. He raised his voice. "They didn't misremember the crime scene!"

Meredith turned to his voice, a hand held up against Helen to quieten her flow of words. "What did you say, Peter?"

"Frankie and Kathy ... they didn't misremember the crime scene. It's a different crime scene."

"What? But the writing was the same as the one in the photograph."

"Yes, it was, but if the visions were a warning ..." He struggled to form his thoughts into a coherent sentence. "If the visions were a warning, they were telling us about a crime that was going to happen, in the *style* of Barry Putchinski!"

"Peter! Do you mean a copy-cat killing?"

"Exactly!" His thoughts were feverish as he remembered the details of the book, Helen and Evangeline's recount of the information they had gathered, or knew about from all the various sources. "Helen! Check in the book. The last two of Barry's victims, where were they killed?"

Helen leafed through the book. Each victim had her own chapter, detailing her abduction, the motivation for her kidnap, her death, and where it took place. "The last two in the book are Betty Jacques and Doris Cruickshank, and they were killed here, in this house."

Helen's face is triumphant, but it quickly falls as Peter says, "But I thought that his last two victims were killed in another house?"

Helen's eyes widen with understanding. "They were! And those women weren't his last two victims. The two women killed at the other property aren't listed in this book!"

"Which means that the last two victims weren't killed by Barry at all, but by a copy-cat killer."

"Seth Golding!" Evangeline sat forward in her chair, taking the book from Helen's grasp.

"Where were the last two victims found? Helen, you said it was at another property."

"Yes, it was." She reached for her folder and searched through the notes. "All I have is a single sentence where it states that his final two victims were found in a cottage ... on the estate!"

"Evangeline?" Peter turned to the owner; all colour had drained from her face as she stared at the book. "Evangeline, Frankie recognised the wallpaper in the photograph in that book, which cottage does it belong to?"

Helen opened the page once again to the image of the bedroom with the iron bedstead and flowered wallpaper.

"It's not my cottage, the walls were never papered in there." Evangeline stared at the photograph. "The woodsman's cottage! There's an old cottage in the woods, at least a mile from here."

"How do we get there?"

CHAPTER THIRTY-EIGHT

Kathy bucked on the bed at the sound of the car's door slamming, but became rigid as heavy footsteps tapped across the kitchen floor. Frankie stooped to the bed, pulling the blindfold from Kathy's eyes. She stared then squeezed her eyes shut, pulling away from the light. Whoever had entered the house continued to move about downstairs. Frankie's heart tripped hard against her sternum, her hands trembling as she reached for Kathy's restraints. The woman remained silent, her eyes staring into Frankie's as they both listened to the footsteps below. Frankie unbuckled the first restraint. The metal clinked and then the leather strap slipped to the floor with a thud. Frankie caught her breath, then reached for the second wrist, fingers fumbling as they trembled.

The first riser creaked. Kathy mewled, her eyes staring. A tear welled at her lashes. With the second restraint unbuckled, Frankie placed it on the bed. Heavy footsteps thudded up the stairs. There was no way that she could undo the restraints before the man – and she was sure it was a man from the heavy footsteps and the grunt of effort with each step up the stairs – arrived at the door.

She scanned the room. Marcy's bed was closest to the door. Ignoring the desperate sight of Marcy's body, she took a massive stride to the end of the bed, and heaved against the frame. It scraped across the floor. The footsteps outside broke into a run. She heaved again, the bed moved, then caught on a raised floorboard. The door swung open with a bang. She heaved again, but the bed was stuck. A broad-shouldered man, completely dressed in black, filled the doorway, a balaclava hid his face. Green eyes, without definition to the outer iris, stared out through the holes. His breathing was laboured—out of breath.

As his eyes narrowed, Frankie grabbed the end of the bed, swinging it round against his legs. The bed swivelled, the headrest thumping into his gut. He buckled with a grunt, but grabbed the bedstead. With a sudden movement, he vaulted over the bed, barrelling into Frankie. His far greater weight knocked her backwards, and she smashed into the wall. Head bursting with pain, and before she had a chance to recover, a thick cable tie was slipped around her wrist and she was strapped to the foot of Kathy's bed.

Chest heaving, the man refastened the restraints on Kathy's wrists, and sat on the bed with Frankie at his feet. He leant back and stroked Kathy's arm. She flinched under his touch. "She looks so much like Doretta Carmichael."

Surprised at the mention of the woman's name, Frankie asked. "Did you know her?"

"No, not personally, but I saw the photographs. And Marcy ... such a beautiful, but conceited woman, she looks so much like Noelle ... I only came back for my book, but ... the resemblance ... I just couldn't resist. It's absolutely not my fault."

"Noelle?"

"Yes, Noelle Anderson, Barry's second victim."

"You seem very knowledgeable," Frankie stated, feigning interest. She had a vague recollection that befriending a captor had saved abducted women's lives. "How do you know she was Barry's second victim?"

"I studied his work in detail. You should read my book, it's very informative."

"You're Seth Golding!"

Silence.

Recognising an opportunity, she said, "*The* Seth Golding?"

"Yes!"

Straining to see the man, his smile was obvious beneath his balaclava. "I thought you were in a maximum-security prison? The whole country is afraid of you!"

He preened. "I was released. I managed to convince the parole board that I was no longer a danger. So pathetic! They have no idea just what drives a man like me." He leant back and stroked along the length of Kathy's arm. "So beautiful. I can see why Barry was attracted to her. Obviously, he told me exactly why he was attracted to her. It's all in my book."

"I'd like to read it ..."

Narrowed green eyes stared out from the black cloth. "And so would I! Barry, that conniving snake, passed it on to a nurse at the prison and I never saw it again. I was going to have it published, I even had a publisher lined up."

"A book like that, surely, would be in the public interest ... a fascinating read?"

"Exactly!"

"Can't you track the nurse down?"

"I have ... to Hemlock House. Can you imagine that? He even left his house to her. Makes you wonder!"

"Wonder?"

"Yes, if they weren't in on it together."

"Oh ..." Frankie's mind whirred. "Then when you get your book back, you must write some extra chapters ... about what you've discovered."

"You're right!"

Frankie scrabbled for something to say; every minute that he talked to her was another minute when she could think of how to escape.

"Have you ... have you done this before?" She gestured to Kathy on the bed?

"Oh, yes, but my last two ladies were my finest; carbon copies of Barry's work. The police never knew it wasn't him." His eyes glittered as he spoke and then he laughed. "He was so angry when I told him." He snickered. "Ironic that the murder he was caught for wasn't actually the one he committed, isn't it?" He traced a finger down Kathy's thigh. "She looks so much like Doretta," he repeated. "She was one of Barry's favourites, he told me that." He glanced at Frankie. "But you! You don't look like any of Barry's girls." Frankie shook her head, unable to think of any response. "I'll have to think of something new for you."

Frankie swallowed, her gut twisting. *Think, Frankie!* "I'd like to see a photograph of Doretta."

He flashed her a glance, narrowing his eyes. "They were in my book!" His jaws clenched and his lips pursed.

"Perhaps I can help you get your book."

"She's got it!"

"Who?"

"Mrs Maybank. It's in the house ... somewhere."

"Then, I think I know where it is."

"Don't' lie! You're just trying to find a way of escaping. One thing I am not, is stupid."

"No! Of course, you're not stupid, Seth. But I'm not lying. I've seen your book, and I know exactly where it is, and I can prove it."

He snorted. "Go on then!"

"Each vic ... girl ... has her own chapter."

"Anyone could have guessed that."

"There are photographs. This bedroom and another of the writing on the wall at Hemlock House."

He stared at her, silent as she continued.

"And the last two victims, they don't have chapters ... because they weren't examples of his ... work."

"And why was that?"

"Because they were yours, but you did such a skilful job of copying him, that the police blamed him and he was convicted of their deaths, but you couldn't bear to add them to his biography. They were your glory, not his."

Seth Golding stood to his full height. "Tell me where it is."

"It's in the attic at the house."

"No, it's not. I've checked."

"Yes, it is! It's in the attic. It was hidden in a chimney breast by Evangeline Maybank. There are bricks that are loose-"

"Which attic?"

"The one above Kathy's room," she lied.

His smile broadened, and despite her terror, Frankie relaxed. Once he left the cottage, she would free herself and help Kathy escape too.

His cheeks lifted in a smile beneath the balaclava. "I've just had a thought."

"Oh, yes?" She attempted a friendly, interested smile.

"Yes, I know exactly what I'm going to do with you."

CHAPTER THIRTY-NINE

The turn-off to the track that would lead them to the woodsman's cottage was further than Evangeline had described and, more than once, Peter had lost hope, and attempted to convince Meredith to turn around. When they finally found the unmarked turnoff, the tarmacked road quickly gave way to a muddy track.

"I'm not sure my car will be able to get any further down here, Peter. It's very churned."

Ahead the track through the trees was rutted. "That's because someone has been using it, recently."

"The cottage is not supposed to be inhabited. Evangeline said that it hasn't been lived in since Barry was imprisoned. The staff were all made redundant and the house and grounds shut up by one of his relatives."

"Perhaps a squatter?"

"Perhaps."

The car's wheels skidded in a deep rut, mud spraying as its wheels slipped, and Meredith shifted down a gear to force the car forward. "Right! That's it." Pulling onto more solid ground, she turned off the engine. "We walk from here. This car wasn't built to go off-road."

They followed the muddy track until the trees gave way to an open space and an old, derelict cottage. A mud-spattered Range Rover was parked to the side.

"That's no squatter."

"Shh!" Meredith reprimanded, pulling Peter behind a tree. "Do you recognise it?"

"No, but whoever it is, is up to no good."

Peter scanned the house. The front door was overgrown with ivy that had grown to the roof and dislodged its tiles. The windows carried decades of grime. Movement drew his eye to an upstairs bedroom where a curtain moved. "I think whoever is in that house must be upstairs."

Meredith followed his eyes to the upstairs room. "It's a draft making the curtains move."

"Yes, but perhaps someone is causing that draft." Peter continued to scan the house, his curiosity increasing with each moment. "I'm going in. Whoever is in there, shouldn't be, and I have just as much right to be in there as they do." He stepped to the next tree.

"Peter!"

"I'm going in Meredith. Why don't you wait in the car for me?"

"No, I'm coming in too."

"Sure, but if they turn nasty, let me do the talking."

Meredith agreed, and followed Peter as he made his way quickly across to the Range Rover and then to the side door. It sat ajar with the dingy kitchen visible between the gap. A blue thermos sat on the counter. "Someone's been camping out here by the look of it." He stepped back to allow Meredith a view of the interior then leant forward, listening for any noise. A thud was followed by a creak of floorboards, and then muffled voices.

Peter pushed the door open and stepped into the kitchen. On the table was an array of knives and what looked like butcher's tools slotted into an unrolled leather pouch. Beside the pouch was a large claw hammer. The tools gleamed in contrast to the grime-spattered table and the dirty floor.

Meredith's fingers closed around Peter's wrist. "Peter," she whispered. "What are those?"

Peter swallowed. The only place he had seen such an assembly of tools was in a film, one that he had no intention of ever watching again. He gestured for Meredith to follow, and made his way to the bottom of the stairs. As he took the first riser, a man shouted in an upstairs room. Peter waited before stepping on the next riser. A woman screamed, her terror curdling. Peter darted back to the kitchen, grabbed the claw hammer, and took great strides up the stairs. He reached the landing within seconds. One door was open and showed a filthy, broken bathroom. Another scream was cut short. Hand clasped around the hammer, Peter grabbed the door's handle and flung it open.

The scene in the room assaulted his senses. A woman lay dead, another was shackled to a bed, and a black figure crouched over another cowering on the floor. The room carried the stench of rot, decay, and death, heavy perfume, and the sourness of fear. The realisation that the woman on the bed had been murdered hit him as he recognised her as Marcy Devereux. At the same time, he saw Kathy, eyes staring in terror, shackled to the bed, her mouth gagged, and then the masked man with his hands around Frankie's throat about to kill again.

Claw hammer in hand he vaulted the bed, slamming it down in an arc as the figure in black turned to him. It caught the man's shoulder, the force of the impact knocking the tool from Peter's hand. The man turned and green eyes wide with pain, stared from the balaclava. His arm hung limp at his side. In one swift move, Peter twisted on his heel and, with all his force, kicked his boot into the man's stomach. The man grunted and buckled, his limp arm swinging as he stumbled across the room. He hit the wall with a thud. Peter followed his advantage, aiming a kick at the man as he slumped to the floor. Quickly scanning the room, he searched for something to tie the man up with. Finding nothing, he placed a heavy foot on the man's back, forcing him to the floor. A moment of inspiration struck, and he reached within his pocket for the spare cable he had stuffed there last night.

With the psychotic man securely shackled, and tied to the radiator beneath the window, he freed Frankie and then Kathy, calling for Meredith to come upstairs.

With Meredith attending to the women, and the police alerted to the situation, he removed the man's balaclava. It was a face he didn't recognise.

"Who are you?"

The man grunted but didn't reply.

"He's Seth Golding," Frankie explained, limping to Peter's side.

"Seth Golding! The man who wrote Putchinski's book?"

"Yes."

"He's not," Kathy's voice rasped, the emotion unhidden. Meredith's arm slipped around the petite woman's shoulder. "He's Doctor Alexander Mansard, the psychologist from the retreat."

The man jerked against his restraints. "I'm both," he shouted. "Both!" He began to rant, shouting about his 'glorious skills', and repeating the names of his victims. Peter took the cloth that had been placed into Kathy's mouth and stuffed it between Seth Golding's teeth. He used the cloth tied around

Kathy's head to gag him. The man continued to jerk, shouting muffled expletives and raving until the noise of the police siren wailed in the near distance.

EPILOGUE

Four Weeks Later
Providence House

As Frankie sipped a cup of tea from her favourite mug, the shadow hovered in the corner of her living room. She ignored the presence and turned instead to Meredith and Peter both of whom were relaxing on her sofa. The kind acceptance in Peter's eyes had returned, for which she was eternally grateful, and he laughed as Meredith finished a story about some faux pas she had committed as a younger woman in her earlier days of exploring wicca and the occult.

"The woman looked at me as though I was insane!" she finished, and Peter roared with laughter, his head thrown back against Frankie's velvet sofa. She couldn't remember a time when she had felt so happy and relaxed, despite the hovering shadow in the corner.

Peter took another bite of the cake Frankie had made in the morning—her signature cake made to the recipe passed down from her Italian grandmother. He bit down, making a noise of enjoyment as cream squeezes from between the sponge.

"So, Frankie, before I was side-tracked by Peter ..." She threw him an amused glance, "we were talking about Hemlock House and Seth Golding."

"That place gave me the shivers as soon as I saw it!"

"It certainly had an ... individual presence."

"You've sorted it though, haven't you Meredith." This spoken through a mouthful of cake.

"I certainly hope so. It took an entire week of cleansing to return the equilibrium of the house. The spirits were so dreadfully distressed."

"And have they gone now?"

"Some, though I suspect not all."

"Some just won't budge, whatever you try." Peter ate the final bite of cake. "Will they, Meredith."

Meredith agreed with a shake of her head.

"That, Miss D'Angelo," Peter replaced his tea plate on the coffee table, "was absolutely delicious."

"My grandmother's recipe. She was Italian. The recipe is a family secret!" Frankie tapped her nose and laughed. "If I told you ..."

Peter returned her laugh, "I'd hate to have the mob on my back!"

"We do originate from Sicily!" Frankie winked then returned her attention to Meredith. "I read about Seth Golding in the newspapers, they didn't make any mention about you, or the haunting at the house."

"No, and that's the way we'd like to keep it. Evangeline wanted absolute discretion, so as far as anyone is aware, we were just guests at the house ..."

"But Peter, it was you who put two and two together. Don't you want recognition for that?"

"Well," his face became serious. "I have the recognition I need." He glanced at Meredith. "Obviously, the publicity would have been great for business ... but we have to respect the client's wishes. There will be other cases that aren't quite so sensitive."

"What a shame, but I guess you're right."

"And how are you, Frankie, after your ordeal?"

Frankie mused for a moment, then said, "Well, since I've realised that my hallucinations are actually sightings, and that I'm not going mad, my anxiety has reduced enormously. And knowing that I helped put a serial killer back where he belongs ..." she shivered, "well, I feel quite proud of that, although it was you and Peter who really did the work there."

"I imagine the police were quite intrusive in their questioning."

"They were, I guess, and the whole spirit thing ... They wrote down everything I told them, but I think they just thought I was some overly stressed celebrity taken over the edge by being kidnapped by a killer." She shivered again. "Poor Marcy!"

The room grew silent, and then Meredith said, "Now, enough of pleasantries! Shall we get back to what we've come here to do today, Frankie?"

Frankie snorted, unsure if the comment was another of Meredith's faux pas, or her way of bucking them out of the gloom that had descended. "I don't know who he is," she said with a glance to the shadow in the corner.

"But we do." Meredith pulled a book from her bag. "His name is Sidney Fletcher. He died here in 1898. He lived here when the house was an orphanage." Meredith took a sip of her own tea then placed it on the coffee table as Frankie turned to the bookmarked page. EMF meter in hand, Peter switched the device on.

"Poor boy!"

"He was," Peter agreed. "It's a sad case."

"Now," Meredith interrupted. "Do you remember what I told you to do?"

"I think so." Frankie took a step towards the shadow whilst spritzing the air with salty water. 'Spirit be gone," she said.

"Good. Now tell him that this is your house," Meredith coached.

"This is my house, and you are not ... welcome here."

The shadow took form, and an opaque apparition of a young boy appeared, his face sorrowful.

But where am I to go? This is my home.

Meredith took her place beside Frankie. "This is her home now. It is time for you to leave."

The boy's head lowered. Meredith lit a tied bunch of sage and wafted the smoke around the room. The boy's form thinned. *But this is my home! Where am I to go?*

Frankie's skin tingled as a well of sadness surged. "He's asking where to go!"

"Tell him to go to the light."

"Go to the light," Frankie repeated.

Meredith continued to spritz the air and wafted the burning sage. The unhappy spectre grew thinner. *I have no one to go to!* Pain rode through Frankie's heart and she grasped Meredith's arm, forcing it to lower. In low tones she said, "I don't think he's harmful ..."

"But he should leave your home, Frankie. He's a nuisance here."

"Oh, I'm not sure I'd call him that. Before I understood just what he was, I was scared, but now ..."

"What are you saying, Frankie?"

"I don't know. It's just that he hasn't got anyone, or anywhere to go."

"He has the other side to go to."

"But ... he's so sad! And this is his home."

"You don't want to complete the cleansing?"

The delicate apparition wavered.

"No, I don't. I'm picking up a great sadness from the boy."

"Yes, I feel that he's lonely."

"I know this sounds crazy, Meredith, but I ... I kind of feel like he belongs here and that – please don't laugh – that I can be here for him." Against the wall, the figure of the boy lifted then lowered, thinned then thickened. Turning to him, Frankie said, "Sidney ..." she glanced at Peter, then Meredith, her cheeks beginning to burn, "if you behave yourself ... you can stay." The boy raised his head, and for the first time, smiled. In the next moment he had gone.

Peter checked the meter. "He's gone! Cheeky blighter didn't even say thank you."

Frankie laughed. "He's just a child."

"Yes, but one that needs to learn some manners."

"Well," Frankie replied with a joyful beat, "perhaps I can teach him."

Peter coughed, and Frankie caught the look he gave to Meredith. She returned a nod, and he said, "Well, did she pass?"

With a grave air, but a glint in her eyes, Meredith returned with, "She certainly did."

Frankie threw Peter a questioning, bemused, frown. He replied with, "How does *Marshall, Blaylock & D'Angelo Psychic Investigations* sound to you, Frankie?'

"Do you mean it?"

A broad smile spread across Meredith's face. "Absolutely, Frankie. Your psychic abilities are strong, and you are exactly the kind of empathic, understanding soul that we need to help us with our work."

"Then yes! I accept."

THE END

Hello! From the Author

Hello, and thank you for reading 'When the Dead Weep'! I have absolutely loved writing the novel, and am very much looking forward to writing more in the series. I have plenty of other stories to write too, and hope you'll join me as I publish them.

My interest in the supernatural comes from personal experience and being brought up in a family that embraces the mysterious. Have you had any supernatural experiences? Are you sensitive to the Others that walk among us? I'd love to know!

If you have enjoyed the book, I would very much appreciate it if you would consider leaving a review. Reviews are crucial for indie authors like me as they encourage Amazon to promote my books, as well as encourage other readers to purchase them.

Also, I love reader feedback. Knowing that you have enjoyed something I've written is a great boost and really motivates me to write more stories that you'll love. To leave a review, just visit the book's page. It won't take long, and doesn't have to be long and detailed; short and sweet is great!

Thank you and happy reading.

JC Blake

Never Miss Another book

For updates about new books, bonus content, special offers, and to stay in touch, visit the author's website and sign up for the newsletter: JCBlake.com

About the Author

JC Blake writes supernatural thrillers and gothic horror novels. This is her debut supernatural thriller, but there are many more to follow.

An English author, JC lives with her four children, husband, and two cats among the flatlands of the Humber estuary where Vikings and Anglo-Saxons once fought, and where, sometimes, on foggy mornings, the sounds of clashing swords can still be heard.

JC loves keeping in touch with her readers and is happy to respond to any questions they have about her books. You can email her, or message her via her Facebook page. Reader comments on her posts make her smile!

• • • •

JCBLAKE@JCBLAKE.COM

Facebook: @JCBlakeAuthor

JC Blake's reader group: Sign up at JCBlake.com

COPYRIGHT

Printed in Great Britain
by Amazon

56569242R00135